PUFFIN BOOKS

About Lucy Brandt

Lucy grew up in Derbyshire and now lives in sunny Brighton with her husband and two children. When she's not writing, she loves cajoling her family into walks across the Sussex countryside, or swimming in the sea.

Lucy also likes inventing new words and trying to sneak them into conversation. You'll need to listen out for that.

Also by Lucy Brandt:

Leonora Bolt: Secret Inventor

Follow Lucy on Twitter and Instagram:
@letlucyb #LeonoraBolt
lucybrandt.com

LUCY BRANDT

LEONORA BOLT

DEEP SEA CALAMITY

ILLUSTRATED BY GLADYS JOSE

PUFFIN

PUFFIN BOOKS

UK | USA | Canada | Ireland | Australia
India | New Zealand | South Africa

Puffin Books is part of the Penguin Random House group of companies
whose addresses can be found at global.penguinrandomhouse.com.

www.penguin.co.uk
www.puffin.co.uk
www.ladybird.co.uk

First published 2022

001

Text copyright © Lucy Brandt, 2022
Illustrations copyright © Gladys Jose, 2022

With thanks to Inclusive Minds for connecting us with
their Inclusion Ambassador network.

With thanks to Salt & Sage for introducing us to
their inclusivity consultants.

The moral right of the author and illustrator has been asserted

Text design by Ken de Silva

Printed and bound in Great Britain by Clays Ltd, Elcograf S.p.A.

The authorized representative in the EEA is Penguin Random House Ireland,
Morrison Chambers, 32 Nassau Street, Dublin D02 YH68

A CIP catalogue record for this book is available from the British Library

ISBN: 978–0–241–43679–0

All correspondence to:
Puffin Books, Penguin Random House Children's
One Embassy Gardens, 8 Viaduct Gardens, London SW11 7BW

For my nieces and nephews

Contents

1
A Little Test Run

It was one of those glorious September days when it feels like summer will never end. The sky was a giddy cartoon blue, the breeze was warm and smelled faintly of bonfires, and the countryside all around the little village of Snorebury-on-Sea glowed gold, as if King Midas himself had sneezed everywhere.

It was the perfect day to launch a submarine out of a tree.

'OK, let me see . . . batteries are fully charged, rudders are in position, periscope is down . . .' Leonora Bolt muttered instructions to herself as she flicked switches on the large control panel in front of her. She was sitting inside the cabin of her six-metre homemade deep-sea explorer, the *Aquabolt*. It was wedged precariously in the remains of the treehouse at number 5, Primrose Lane.

'Air pressure – check. Fuel levels – check. Otter seatbelt – oh no, hang on . . .'

Perched on a cashmere cushion beside Leonora was her pet otter, Twitchy Nibbles. His bright eyes fixed her with a look of dismay. His nostrils flared. Leonora leaned over and tickled the pale bib of fur beneath his chin with her oily fingers. Then she strapped him in.

'Hey, don't worry, Twitch. This'll be a piece of cake.'

Twitchy let out a low, harrumphing growl

and buried his head beneath his paws as Leonora completed her last-minute inspections. As she adjusted valves and clicked dials, she could feel excitement fizzing away inside her like a Jacuzzi full of sherbet.

Everything was ready for the test run. She'd calculated all the angles and velocities. She'd rehearsed the route 327 times in her mind. The wind speed was low, and the tide was high. This was going to be absolutely perfect.

Leonora couldn't afford any more mishaps. Last night, when she'd been in the submarine up in the treehouse, experimenting with ultraviolet light, she'd made all the local squirrels glow in the dark.* They'd lit up the little garden like Christmas lights. Of course, she'd turned the UV off again the moment she'd

---

* No squirrels were harmed during the making of this chapter. Some squirrels glow bubble-gum pink under UV light. Also, wombat poo is cube-shaped. Keep reading for more incredible animal science!

realized – but what if the neighbours had seen? It was a silly mistake. A close call. She *had* to be more discreet.

BRUUN!! BRRUNNN!! BRUUU-UUNNNNNG!!!

Leonora turned the ignition and the diesel-electric engine roared to life. Great swirls of grey smoke filled the garden. Tree branches shuddered, launching leaves high into the sky. The motor made a strange **HACK**, **HACK**, **HACK** noise like a hoarse donkey coughing up hay . . . but then it sputtered off again.

'Oh no, what is it *this* time?' Leonora sighed and scrambled out of her seat. She turned and opened a large metal compartment behind her. 'I'm so useless at fixing this,' she mumbled, prodding the engine inside with a screwdriver. Her fizziness was starting to get flattened by anxiety.

You see, Leonora wasn't *supposed* to be

launching a subaquatic vehicle out of a tree. Or illuminating the local wildlife. She was *supposed* to be doing the exact opposite of that – lying low, keeping her head down, *blending in*. For Leonora Bolt was a nine-year-old girl in hiding.

Now, in fact, Leonora thought she was pretty good at this hiding malarkey. Not too long ago, she'd been hiding on tiny Crabby Island just off the coast. OK, not *hiding* exactly. More like being forcibly hidden, imprisoned there from the age of three by her ghastly uncle, Lord Luther Brightspark. He was a mediocre professor who'd become ridiculously rich and famous by stealing Leonora's remarkable inventions. And he'd stolen her parents too, so that Leonora had grown up her whole life thinking she was an orphan.

Recently, though, her life had been transformed. It had all started when Jack, a boy from Snorebury, which was on the mainland, had accidentally found himself marooned on her island. Together with Leonora's housekeeper, Mildred, and the hapless ferryman Captain Spang, they'd escaped her uncle's clutches. Then Leonora had discovered that her parents were alive and being held hostage at a mysterious ocean location. Hence the submarine. Leonora was going to get her family back and *nothing* was going to stand in her way.

Leonora rubbed her forehead with her wrist, leaving a dirty smudge. Could the problem be the fuel injection pump, or clogged air filters? She'd need to investigate, which meant more delays.

She shivered, refusing to think about the possibility of her uncle finding her before she'd finished. The last time she'd seen him, she'd scuppered his lifelong plans to own a powerful new technology – a human emotion formula. She'd banished him back to Crabby Island using an amazing teleporting machine she'd invented: the Switcheroo. Foiling his wicked schemes had been Leonora's greatest-ever achievement. She swore she would *never* let him win. She knew, though, that if he was still alive, he was going to be angrier than a whole sackful of scorpions.

That's why Leonora was now living undercover in Snorebury (a designated World Weariness Site and Area of Outstanding Natural Monotony, winner of the Most Tedious Village award for 463 years running). It was a picture-postcard place, where people ironed their lawns, polished their dustbins and hoovered their children, a humdrum haven where she hoped her uncle couldn't find her – although she worried that the dangerously boring residents *might* start to notice things like neon rodents adorning the hedgerows. Or marine vessels appearing out of the blue. The speed of light was 299,792,458 metres per second, which Leonora calculated was only half the speed of village gossip. In short, a few more failed attempts and her cover would be blown.

'Well, I think I need some spare parts,' she said, shutting the engine compartment again. 'Looks like launch day's postponed, Twitch.'

Twitchy's ears pricked up. His whiskers stopped wobbling. Leonora unclunked his seatbelt and gave him a cuddle. Then she pulled

out a silver locket on a chain round her neck. Inside was a faded photograph of her parents. They were holding hands and smiling into the camera. 'I'm coming for you,' she whispered, pressing the picture to her lips, 'no matter what.'

Snapping the magnetic clasp shut again, Leonora stashed the locket next to her heart. 'Looks like you'll be starting school with me tomorrow after all,' she said, gently stroking Twitchy's head. He squeaked, hopped from her arms and tried to burrow under his cushion.

Leonora was just about to coax him out again when she heard something that made all the hairs on her neck **SPROING!** to attention. Footsteps were clanking overhead. *Who could have got up there?* she thought. She heard someone trying to prise open the submarine's hefty steel hatch, and then suddenly a voice said, 'Aha! Found you!'

2
Non-Uniform Day

'Ooof, Jack, don't sneak up on me like that.' Leonora pushed open the submarine's hatch to let him in. Her heart felt like it was performing a drum solo in her chest. 'What happened to our special code – five short knocks?'

'Oh, soz. Didn't mean to make you jump,' he said, following her down the ladder. He landed on the patchwork rug beside her with a soft thud. A bulging carrier bag swung from his arm.

'I tried our knock but you couldn't hear me over the engine,' said Jack, 'which you could probably hear in *Australia* by the way. Remember we talked about this, Leo? You're supposed to be keeping your head down.'

Leonora winced. 'I know . . . I'm trying my best,' she said.

'Well, anyway, this is looking . . . *cosy*,' he said, gazing about. He flashed her a lopsided grin that was more gap than tooth.

Leonora smiled back. Her interior design style (if she had such a thing) could be described as 'shabby U-boat chic'. Two comfy benches ran either side of the hull with pull-down bunks above. Shelves were lined with vintage tools (which looked like they'd been salvaged from Victorian times). And Captain Spang, an expert needle-wielder, had sewn cushions and throws in a range of luxurious fabrics.

'I was preparing for the test run,' said Leonora, wiping her greasy hands on a velvet quilt.

'Is it ready for that?'

'Nearly. Just need to fix the engine and finish the Shooter-Scooter 6.0.'

'The shooter what?'

'Just a little something I've built. I'll show you.'

Leonora moved through the main cabin and yanked open a door at the rear of the submarine. Behind it was a cramped storage space that contained a round contraption: a mobility scooter stuffed inside what looked like an oversized hamster ball.

Jack frowned. 'Hmm, what's that?' he asked, peering over her shoulder.

'A *submersible*. It's a sort of underwater boat that lets you go really deep in the ocean. Took a lot of waterproofing and a new engine and breathing system. Should be safe to a depth of 1,317.6 metres, give or take.'

'OK. And how deep does the sub go?'

'*Crush* depth approximately 528.5 metres.'

'*Crush* depth?' Jack's voiced jumped an octave.

'Yeah. That's how far down you are when the hull collapses due to the immense water pressure. Don't worry though. I've made depth gauges out of those digital alarm clocks I got at the charity shop.'

'Depth gauges?'

'They measure how deep the sub is diving, so it'll be OK. The plan is, I'm going to roll her down Neat Street to the harbour, sail around Immaculate Bay, then I'll hide her underneath the fishing boats.'

'Wait . . . you want to drive a submarine through Snorebury?'

'Yep.'

'In broad daylight?'

'Uh-huh.'

'With a – a pair of *skateboards* as wheels?'

'We'll take the back streets.'

'Oh, no worries then!'

Leonora finally noticed the hysterical edge in Jack's tone. When he put it like that, she supposed it did sound a little . . . *challenging*. If the test run went well, they'd soon be sailing the sub hundreds of miles to a bleak and treacherous patch of the Unspecific Ocean. (She decided not to mention that bit yet.)

'Look, it'll be fine,' she reassured him. 'I've got peanut butter sandwiches and 6 kilograms of emergency jelly babies. I'm not totally bonkers.' Leonora had only discovered the existence of sweets a few weeks ago and she'd built up a huge stockpile for the journey.

Jack didn't say anything. *Why doesn't he look more impressed?* she thought. He was fixing her with such an intense look that she suddenly felt deeply unsure of everything. Of course, the plan was ridiculous. And dangerous. The whole idea was as sensible as trying to tickle a grizzly bear.

But what other plan did she have? Her only link to her parents was the ocean coordinates she'd taken from Uncle Luther. She *had* to go there and search for clues.

'It's OK,' she said. 'I can do this on my own, you know.'

Jack sighed. 'No, Leo. You can't go without me. We're a *team*. I swore I'd help you find your family, just like you helped me get back to mine. Besides, you'll need someone to calm *him* down,' he said, pointing out of the viewport at Twitchy, who was now in the garden below, leaving another little otter deposit for Leonora to step in. It was something he'd been doing quite a lot lately, and she thought she knew why.

'Twitch doesn't want to come,' she admitted. 'He's been picking up bad vibrations, weird undersea sounds, when he's been swimming down in the harbour.' Leonora removed a piece of paper from her pocket and handed it to Jack.

'I made these read-outs using the tremors from his whiskers. Not sure what they mean though.'

Jack stared at the wonky graph drawn on the paper, and they gave each other an uneasy look. 'Beats me,' he said, handing the paper back, 'but something tells me we're going to find out. Oh yeah,' he added, 'nearly forgot. Mum told me to give you these clothes from my sisters for school tomorrow,' and he thrust the carrier bag into Leonora's hand.

Inside was a starched purple skirt, a purple jumper and a stiff orange blazer. They had all the style, comfort and practicality of the wooden trousers she'd once invented.

'I'm not wearing *those*,' she said, frowning. 'Won't I need a new lab coat? Safety goggles? Maybe a full-body thermal radiation protection suit?'

Jack looked confused. 'Umm, nope, don't think so.'

Leonora narrowed her eyes. So *this* was what he'd meant when he'd talked about a uniform. Jack had been extremely vague (some might say outrageously unhelpful) on all the details about school and, as Leonora had never been to school before, she had her own ideas of what it would be like.

In her mind, she had conjured up a gleaming modern building staffed by the world's greatest thinkers. At her imaginary school, every classroom was filled with the latest laboratory

equipment and astonishing machines. She couldn't wait to have her own workshop, with all the band saws, angle grinders and plunge routers a kid could wish for! Lessons would range from the fairly standard (you know, classroom tornado simulations, cyborg

plant growth, rollercoaster design and testing, five-dimensional chess . . .) to the *slightly* more advanced (anti-gravity Thursdays, space-rocket test driving, time travel for beginners . . .). There would obviously be daily lectures on bending space-time, practical sessions involving the development of flying flip-flops and invisibility serums. And who would teach her? Leonora often thought about her mother's favourite teacher, Professor Echo. Perhaps Leonora would be lucky enough to have a mentor like that too. Someone kind and incredible who would teach her all the wonders of the universe.

'All right, I'll wear it,' said Leonora, feeling a fresh rush of anticipation, 'but I'm making a few adjustments. And come on, what's school really like?'

Jack shrugged. 'It's like . . . *forever.*'

Leonora grinned. That sounded perfect. As she set about altering the awful uniform, she pictured herself with her new classmates, learning loads and doing clever things. She heard the bright tinkle of approving laughter from her teachers, already saw the gold stars, the A-grades. Yes, Leonora was sure that school was going to be unbelievably, undeniably, totally amazing.

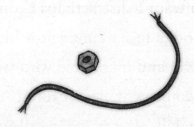

3
School's Out

'Laura Drumble-Splang? Laura Drumble? Oh, for heaven's sake – **LAURA!**'

Leonora was so distracted she almost forgot to answer to her fake name.

'Hmm . . . yep?'

She had been busy reading the lesson timetable, aghast. It was the middle of morning registration (and somehow she was already in the middle of a big telling-off).

'It's not *Hmm, yep*! It's *Yes, Miss Clink*!'

Leonora turned back to the timetable. Was *this* what the children of Snorebury studied at school? Because Leonora was sure she'd never seen anything so eye-poppingly, teeth-itchingly, brain-rinsingly dull.

9.00 a.m.

Sitting Nicely

10.00 a.m.

PE – Expressive Ribbon Dance

11.00 a.m.

The History of Teapots 1819–1972

12.00 p.m.

Luncheon

1.00 p.m.

Delicate Handkerchief Embroidery Level 476

2.00 p.m.

Crayon Maintenance

2.30 p.m.

Colouring INSIDE the Lines

Leonora looked up to find her new teacher, Miss Clink, glaring at her over half-moon spectacles. 'Well, Laura? I'm waiting, young lady.'

Chairs scraped back as her new classmates turned to gawk at her too. Leonora wasn't used to people staring at her. She wasn't used to people full stop (end of sentence).

'Um, sorry, Miss Clink,' Leonora stammered. She tugged at the starched collar digging into her neck. Her woolly jumper felt itchier than a bath full of gnats. And she could hear Twitchy grumbling where she'd concealed him inside her desk drawer. (She prayed he wasn't leaving an otter deposit in there too.)

'That's more like it,' said the teacher, hopping out from behind her desk. She was a small, sparrow-like woman with a beaky nose and permanently pained expression. 'Now, class, I'm sure we want to make Laura feel welcome on her first day.'

'*Yeeesss, Miiiiss Clii-iinnk,*' came the chorus.

'So what better way is there than getting to know her? Laura, you're our Star of the Week! Come to the front, dear, and we'll ask you some questions.'

Leonora felt a lump forming in her throat as though she'd tried to swallow a grand piano. Sideways. Her eyes slid about the room in panic.

'Do I have to?'

'Yes, dear. It's what all new starters do. Come on up and tell us everything.'

Everything? She wasn't allowed to tell them anything! Zero. Zilch. Nought. Nada.

Very, very (very) slowly, Leonora pushed back her chair and walked to the front of the class. Jack, who was sticking to their cover story and pretending they didn't know each other, gave her a covert wink. *Keep calm*, it seemed to say. *Don't say too much.*

It was at this moment that Leonora's tie escaped from where she'd gaffer-taped it to her

neck and fluttered to the floor. Even worse, as she walked, the tool belt she'd concealed under her skirt kept clanking like a knight's armour. This was super annoying because Leonora was sure she was only carrying the absolute essentials: four chisels, a blowtorch and her brand-new **Sonic Headteacher Demobilizer** (a state-of-the-art amplifier and loudspeaker with a range of distracting sounds to get her out of trouble).

Leonora made her way to the front. She

swallowed hard and turned to face the class.

'Right. I'll go first,' said Miss Clink, perching on a nearby desk. 'Now then, what's your favourite hobby?'

Leonora's dark eyes darted about the classroom at all the unfamiliar faces. She felt her cheeks burn. Hobby – hobby – think of something, *anything* –

'Spot welding!' she blurted out.

Silence. Twenty-nine pairs of blank eyes gazed back at her. Jack gave an encouraging nod. The air thickened like bad custard. A boy near the front thrust his hand up.

'Yeah, so what's, like, your favourite book?'

'Um, that's a hard one,' she mumbled. 'I'd have to say *Weather Warrior* by Tarrigan Flampstand.'

There was a stifled giggle at the back of the class. Then another and another.

'So who's your favourite pop band?' shouted

a girl with pretty pigtails and a mean smirk.

Leonora didn't know any pop bands. She'd only ever listened to Uncle Luther's relentless harpsichord music. True, Captain Spang played experimental trans-global freeform fusion folk-funk, but that was best enjoyed with earplugs. She'd have to improvise.

'Erm, the – the – um – the White Boards?'

The class erupted into great peals of laughter. Jack turned and glowered at everyone. Leonora dug her nails into her palms. This was the single most embarrassing moment of her life. She felt about as welcome as a slug in a sandwich. The dial on her newly designed CringeMatic 3000 would be tipping from Light Tomato Blush, past Sweaty Purple Awkwardness, to Red-Hot Lava Tsunami of Shame.

'Now, settle down, class!' urged Miss Clink, coming to Leonora's rescue. 'That's certainly not a proper Snorebury Primary welcome, is it?' she added, giving the gigglers a stern glare. 'It sounds as though Laura has some *intriguing* interests. You can sit back down, dear.'

Leonora sighed with relief. But before she could move, there was a sudden rap at the classroom door. A large man with a sharp suit and black hat stepped into the room. 'Apologies, Miss Clink,' he said gruffly as he surveyed the children. 'Is there a Leonora Bolt in this class?'

Leonora froze, willing herself to stay calm. She locked eyes with Jack, who flushed red.

'Not in here, Mr . . . I'm sorry, I didn't catch your name?' Miss Clink frowned. Instead of a name badge, the man wore a pale blue lapel pin inscribed with one word: *Iceheart*.

'Oh, my mistake, not to worry,' the man said quickly, as he backed out and closed the door again.

Miss Clink paused and shook her head. She gestured for Leonora to return to her desk, but as Leonora finally regained control of her jelly-legs and stepped forward the **Sonic Headteacher Demobilizer** slipped from her tool belt. It hit the floor with a massive **FLONK** before rolling away, lights flickering.

There were gasps from the class. Children jumped up to get a closer look at the remarkable gadget, and Pigtail Girl stopped smirking and looked impressed, all of which made Leonora feel two things at once –

1. Pleased that she'd broken the ice.
2. Seized by UTTER BUM-FLAPPING PANIC!

– because Leonora realized she'd made a terrible mistake. Now she saw that Snorebury Primary wasn't ready for technology this advanced. It would blow their minds – and her cover too!

She lurched forward to recover her machine, chasing it between legs and under chairs. She dived sideways across the room, upsetting desks, stacks of books, pots of pencils and plants, and landed with a thunderous **THWUMP** in Book Corner. The whole class **YAAAAAAAYED** as if this was the most exciting thing that had ever happened at school. Which, of course, it absolutely was.

'Laura, this will not do!' cried Miss Clink, hopping over and picking up the device with a baffled look. 'I will not tolerate this sort of disruption. Or . . . *toys* in class. You'll see me later – for detention!'

From where she lay upside down in Book Corner, Leonora cracked open one eye and surveyed the destruction she'd left behind her. She then peeled her grubby legs off the bookcase and rolled the right way up. The mess looked even worse.

I've blown it, she thought. Her first day at school and she was already the talk of the class. She should have checked with Jack before she brought her stupid machine along. This wasn't Show and Tell. It was a Hide and SHUSH!

And *who* was that man in the sharp suit? Why was he looking for her? There was no time to wonder about that, as she got awkwardly to her feet, because an almighty **TRRRIIIIIIINGGG** sound suddenly vibrated in the air all around. Leonora guessed Miss Clink must have unknowingly activated high-pitched frequencies from the SHD (the **Sonic Headteacher Demobilizer** – keep up). The emergency glass shattered in the small red box beside the door and the fire alarm began to blare.

4
A Brown Cloud

Children streamed out of their classrooms and on to the playing field and lined up in chattering rows. A fire engine **BLLLAAARPED** its way through the school gates, lights flashing. Meanwhile, a cloud of noxious brown gas appeared in the sky like a huge airborne cowpat.

Leonora hurried to the back of the class line with her head down, trying to conceal an otter-shaped bulge beneath her blazer. She glanced sideways to find Jack beside her.

'So much for your low profile,' he whispered.

'I know. Why didn't you tell me about all the questions?'

'Didn't I? Soz. Detention with Clinkerbell on your first day though – wow! Must be a new school record.'

'Yeah, amazing, thanks. And who was that man? He knew my real name.' Leonora stayed hunched over, trying to make herself as small as possible.

'Dunno. He's not one of our usual teachers.' Jack stood on tiptoes and scanned the playground. 'I think he's gone . . . that was so weird though.'

The children watched boggle-eyed as squads of hefty firemen raced across the playground and through the canteen doors. Thirty seconds later they came bowling back out again, noses running like snot taps, eyes streaming with tears. Then an army truck appeared, squeezing down the little country lane. Figures in protective suits jumped out and made their way into the building. Headteacher Trevor Fandango started bleating into a loudhailer –

'Children, this is not a drill. Repeat: not a

drill! There's been . . . erm . . . a gas leak in the canteen. We're being evacuated. The autumn fete will now take place on the village green on Saturday. All classes dismissed!'

An immense cheer went up from the children. And Leonora felt relieved too. She'd dodged expressive ribbon dance, whatever sweet horror that was. And if there was a strange man asking for her by her real name at school, then school was the *last* place she wanted to be. She nodded to Jack and they were swept along in the tide of kids rushing towards the gates.

'Whoa – what did your machine *do*?' asked Jack.

'No idea. Didn't think it could burst gas pipes,' she replied.

'Well, you're probably the most popular kid in school now,' said Jack with a grin. 'Nice one.'

Leonora returned a cautious smile and followed Jack up the village high street, Twitchy hopping at her heels. A couple of Jack's younger siblings scampered past on their way home. Leonora was still bewildered by the concept of siblings, since she didn't have any and Jack had ten. His house was always filled with laughter, bickering and the exquisitely awful screeching sounds of bad violin practice. It was probably why Jack had slept over at Leonora's house thirty-seven nights in a row. In her opinion, this was technically called 'moving in'.

Because of her secluded upbringing, Leonora was confused by lots of other things too. Such as ironing. And deckchairs. And clogs, electric toothbrushes, musical theatre, the internet, why on earth anyone thinks clowns are a good idea, Easter eggs, weekends, hummus and the point of golf. (All of which Jack had been doing his best to explain.)

They carried on past the village shops – Basil Crumb's Buns, Knit-Wits Wool Shop,

Tim's Trims – and came to a stop outside Fun & Games. Leonora looked up at the toyshop's cheerful window display and felt her insides drop, as if she'd tripped over her own shoelaces.

'Leo, come on, don't upset yourself,' said Jack, but Leonora wasn't listening.

Her heart thumped as she gazed up at the window. It was stuffed full of fantastic gifts, like Satellite Spyglasses and Hover-Beanbags, Solar-Powered Super Visors and Ever-Expanding Sea Trampolines, Pump-Action Flannels, Holographic Hair Gel and Disco Teeth. A magnificent treasure trove of novelty and delight – but it made Leonora feel sick. The sign behind the gadgets read *Brightspark Industries*, the name of her Uncle Luther's company, but Leonora, not her uncle, had invented *every single one* of them. The window display also featured a poster of a tall, bony man with shiny black hair and a smile about as real as tinsel. To

the rest of the world he was a beloved celebrity –
a genius – *Mr Fun*. But to Leonora and Jack he
was a dangerous man: her evil Uncle Luther.

She felt Twitchy rub his nose against her
ankle. Jack tugged on her sleeve.

'Don't worry,' he whispered. 'You're safe.'

Despite Jack's reassurances, Leonora felt the
old panic rising inside her. The familiar sting of
fear mixed with outrage. To her, Uncle Luther

was about as fun as sunburn. He had all the charm of gastric flu. She thought again about the man at the door of the classroom. *Did Uncle Luther send him?*

'Yeah, I'm sure you're right,' she said at last, forcing herself to look away from the creepy poster. There was a long pause, then she asked, 'How much money have you got on you?'

Jack emptied his pockets and held out some coins. 'Hmm, not much.'

'Mind if I borrow some?' she asked. 'Might need to haggle a bit –' and before he could complain, Leonora had swiped the coins and dashed a few doors up the street into what had become her dream shop. It was DIY heaven: Sprocket & Daughters, the hardware shop.

Leonora stepped inside and breathed in the musty scent of sawdust, axle grease and old men's beards. From floor to ceiling were boxes filled with nails and nubbits and noggins and brackets and flackets and widgets and dorgles and screw eyes and spronks and fangles and tacks and snocks. A bit like a pick 'n' mix for engineers. Ten minutes later she re-emerged, arms bulging.

'You spent my sweet money on *that*?' Jack protested.

Leonora grinned. 'Of course! Got some total bargains. Now we've not got boring school, you can help me fix the fuel pump. And recalibrate the hydrodynamic control fins.'

Jack's pale eyebrows bumped into each other. 'The what?'

'The steering bits. I'll show you.'

Jack looked puzzled, but he helped Leonora carry her stash of materials along the high street and up the steep hill. Before long they arrived at Primrose Lane, a row of pastel-coloured cottages with clipped garden hedges and identical doors. They say that home is where the heart is. Would this ever feel like home to Leonora? She doubted it. The only home she'd ever known was Crabby Island . . . but *he* was there. And her heart? Well, that was floating somewhere out in the distant ocean, with her parents. And if she was going to find them, she had to be discreet. Stay under the radar. *Blend in*.

Reaching the gate, they dumped the supplies in the neat front garden. Then something important occurred to Leonora. She'd been so focused on surviving her first day at school that she hadn't put two and two together. Or even one and one together. How could she have forgotten? Mildred also had a big day. She had started a new job.

As one of the school's dinner ladies.

5
Echo Location

SNIIIIIIFFF, **PHLAAAARP!**

Leonora pushed open the dainty cottage door to hear the trumpety sound of Mildred blowing her nose.

'We're home!' Leonora called. 'Hey, Millie, what's wrong?'

Mildred was bustling about the minuscule kitchen, mincing, mashing, roasting, poaching and generally annihilating ten awful ingredients at once. She was wearing a stained yellow apron and a disgruntled look.

'Oh, sweetheart,' she said, 'I've – I've been *sacked*!'

'No way,' said Jack, gamely attempting a surprised face.

'There was an, er, *incident* at school . . . my lovely conker casserole gots a bit out of hand!'

'That brown cloud was from *your* stew? I thought *I'd* set the alarms off!' Leonora frowned. 'We're supposed to be keeping a low profile, Millie.'

'I knows,' said Mildred, guiltily. 'The other dinner lady, Brenda Spaniel, completely over-reacted. Bossy old so-and-so. She's had it in for me since day one!'

'This is day one,' said Jack.

'I know more about cooking hot dinners than she's *had* hot dinners,' Mildred muttered, folding her arms. 'And she's got

Angus in trouble too!'

Captain Spang came clanging into the kitchen, guitar in hand. His billowing white shirt was askew and his flowery cravat was undone. Leonora and Jack stared in confusion at his leg, which had a weighty metal disc attached to it, like one of those used for clamping illegally parked cars.

'Och, I wasnae going to tell you kiddlywinks,' he said, squeezing past them and plonking himself on to a chair with a dramatic flourish, 'but ma village pub tour got cancelled last week. The Ham and Anchor, the Cat and Flannel, the Barmy Badger – all my gigs have been pulled!'

'Wow, *really*?' said Jack.

'So's I thought I'd earn some extra money,' continued Captain Spang. 'But,' he said, waving at his leg, 'I got clamped for busking in the village square after Brenda Spaniel reported me. She wouldnae ken real music if it painted itself blue and tap-danced into her ears.'

Leonora winced, remembering meeting Brenda (a formidable woman in tweed, so cross

with the world she appeared to have sprained her own face) on their recent moving-in day. Brenda's thoughtful house-warming gift was a list of village rules as long as an anaconda's sleeping bag. They included:

1. No CHEWING GUM.
2. No LAUGHING ON A WEDNESDAY.
3. No BALL GAMES ON THE VILLAGE GREEN.
4. No GREEN BALLS IN THE VILLAGE HALL.
5. No SPEEDING — MAXIMUM SPEED 0.0000000003 MPH.
6. No SKATEBOARDING.
7. No INFERNAL POPULAR MUSIC.
8. AND ABSOLUTELY NO SILLY NONSENSE!

Now every time Leonora turned a corner in Snorebury, she seemed to bump into Brenda and her regulations.

'Well, I'm sure we can find you both new jobs,' said Leonora, trying her best to sound convincing, but just then the radio on the sideboard switched to a news bulletin and drowned her out.

Good afternoon. These are the headlines at eleven o'clock, said the newsreader. *Police in Mavenbridge say they are trying to trace the whereabouts of a leading academic. Acoustics scholar Professor Kenneth Echo went missing from St Marmalade's College five days ago. Detectives are appealing for any witnesses who may have seen the professor to come forward . . .*

Leonora's ears swivelled round like satellite dishes. Her stomach turned over.

'Professor Echo . . . *missing?*' she said, staring at the radio in astonishment.

'Wasn't he your mum's tutor when she was at SIG?' asked Jack.

'Shhhh,' said Mildred, flinching, 'keep your voices down, sweethearts. We can't mention . . . *the society*.' She proceeded to hurry about the kitchen and living room, shutting windows, closing curtains. She even put a lid on the goldfish bowl for good measure.

'Sorry,' said Leonora, itching with impatience, 'but why didn't SIG tell us Professor Echo was missing? Why are they keeping us in the dark?' Leonora's mind was now in hyperdrive as she thought about SIG – the Society of Ingenious Geniuses – in Mavenbridge. It was a secret group of the world's top inventors and all-round brainboxes. They created awesome technologies to solve the most complex challenges facing humankind. Mildred had worked as a superfood scientist when Leonora's parents were students there. She'd taught Leonora's mum, who'd gained a SIG scholarship, much to Luther's envy. One day he'd got his revenge, luring Leonora's parents on a fake Arctic research expedition and taking them prisoner.

'They're not keeping us in the dark,' whispered Mildred, in the now gloomy living room. 'Professor Puri would have warned us if something was wrong. She and the SIG team are on constant surveillance in case Luther ever comes back.'

'Yeah,' said Jack, 'but some guy was looking for Leo at school earlier.'

Mildred gasped. 'Looking for you? Why didn't you tells us?! Oh no, this isn't right at all.'

'Aye, something smells fishy,' agreed Captain Spang, picking up a cod-and-marzipan sandwich from a plate on the sideboard.

Leonora gazed from Mildred to Jack, to Captain Spang and to Twitchy. She felt a dreadful sinking feeling, like a flimsy dinghy taking on water.

'I don't think this is our safe house any more,'

she said. 'We've got to get out of here, *fast*. So I need to fix the sub!'

For a second Mildred looked as though she might protest, but then she said, 'Don't need to tell us twice, sweetheart. And don't think I haven't noticed that sub you've been building. It's bloomin' marvellous! Do you wants some conker gas for fuel?'

Leonora thought for a moment. Weapons-grade culinary biofuel was Professor Mildred Dribble's speciality. It was her pungent fermented caviar that had powered their daring airborne escape from Crabby Island a few weeks before.

'Not this time, Millie,' she said, giving her a determined nod. 'Just pack your things. We're leaving on the next tide!'

6
A Fete with Destiny

Far too early the next morning, Leonora, Jack, Twitchy, Mildred and Captain Spang sat bleary-eyed inside the submarine's cabin, preparing for launch: round two, the sequel.

The *Aquabolt* was still up in the tree in the garden, but Leonora had worked around the clock to fix the sub's temperamental engine. The final touch was to dismantle the clock and use its cogs to secure her triple-decker periscope in place. At last everything was ready.

'You're *sure* there isn't an easier route?' said Jack, nervously looking out of the viewport (recycled washing-machine door). The harbour slipway was just a titchy speck at the bottom of the steep hill far below.

'Not really,' said Leonora. 'But it'll be totally fine. Have I failed you before?'

'Just that time you crashed our hot-air balloon into that hundred-foot clock tower.'

'Oh yeah . . .'

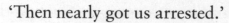

'Then nearly got us arrested.'

'Hmm, OK, that was a *bit* dangerous. But this'll be much easier. For starters, we're not flying anywhere. Unless I've really messed up the sums!'

Jack rolled his eyes and carried on looking suspicious – and Twitchy joined in, which made Leonora feel a stab of guilt. She hadn't mentioned the list of things that could go wrong. It was only short:

Item 1: The whole sub could disintegrate on impact with water and squish us to absolute bits.
Item 2: See Item 1.

As captain, however, Leonora felt she needed to maintain an air of breezy confidence, so she busied herself checking valves and resetting gauges. Green lights blinked, needles on dials spun round. Their breath kept steaming up the viewport.

After several more minutes, she said, 'Right, let's do this. Prepare for launch!'

Twitchy squarked. Jack pulled on his shin pads and goalie gloves. Mildred adjusted her flying goggles. And Captain Spang thumbed his guitar strings, playing a sombre sea shanty about some guy called Davy Jones and his locker. It wasn't helping to lighten the mood.

Leonora turned the ignition key and there was a deep rumbling noise as the engine started. The submarine started to shudder and vibrate all around them. She released the brake and it tipped forward –

SCRRROOOOORRRFFFF!!!!

Leonora felt a rush of pure exhilaration as the sub slid smoothly down the forty-five-degree ramp she'd constructed from a playground slide. It bounced on to the pavement,

skateboard wheels creaking
under its heavy hull. Then it started
to pick up speed, rolling a little (actually loads)
faster than Leonora had estimated. Past ordered
rows of fishermen's cottages they sailed, and on
down towards the harbour below.

It was just at this moment that Leonora had
a flashback to her first (and only) day at school.
A thought snapped like an old fan belt inside
her brain –

'Jack – what day is it?' she shouted, over the
violent clattering.

'It's **SAAAAT-TUR-TUR-DAAAAY!**' stuttered Jack, his teeth shaken by all the vibrations.

'And what did Mr Fandango say was happening today?'

'The autumn fete, on the village green –'

'AARRRRRRHHHHHGGGHHH!!!!!'

A large marquee decorated in bunting suddenly loomed into view at the bottom of the hill, with dozens of people preparing for the fete. What kind of utter barbarians were awake this early on a Saturday morning? The PTA, that's who, and Leonora definitely hadn't factored prize marrows or cream teas into her launch plans.

'Leo, we're heading straight for the fete! You've got to stop!' cried Jack.

'I know, but I can't – everything's jammed!'

They were now
careering down the hill,
faster and faster. The sub was like a
fish out of water (or a berserk mechanical shark
out of water). Everyone clung on for dear life
as cushions and cookies ricocheted around the
cabin. Leonora frantically pulled levers, but it
was impossible to steer the craft. Down Neat
Street they raced, juddering and lurching this

way and that. Instead of heading towards the harbour, the *Aquabolt* jerked sharply to the left.

What happened next wasn't in slow motion, like you see in films. No. It was in double-quick time and full, lurid, technicolour detail.

The submarine ploughed headlong through the middle of the ill-fated fete. People shrieked and dived out of the way as it burst the bouncy castle, barrelled through the apple-bobbing, rammed the raffle, scuttled the skittles, and – finally! – came to a halt slap bang in the middle of the baking marquee.

'You know when you said it would be totally fine?' mumbled Jack, uncurling himself from the brace position. 'Well, that wasn't.'

'No, but we're OK,' said Mildred, who was wedged sideways beneath the bunks.

'Aye, never better,' agreed Captain Spang, shaking broken biscuit bits from his beard.

'Ooof, sorry, everyone,' said Leonora,

staring at the sheered-off metal stick she was now clutching. 'Think the handbrake needs adjusting.'

For the next few moments they all sat quietly dazed. The viewport was so smothered in buttercream icing that no one could see out. Leonora finally plucked up the courage to flick on the wipers. Through two clean triangles they could just make out members of the Nit-Picking Litter Committee and the Bored Village Board. They did not look pleased.

Leonora felt a wave of shame (CringeMatic 3000 reading: Clammy Scarlet Humiliation). It was closely followed by absolute panic. What if she'd damaged the sub? They couldn't stop now. They just *had* to get to the slipway – and get out to sea!

'Let me do the talking,' said Jack. 'I'll say we're entering the go-kart race or something.'

'There's no time to explain,' said Leonora.

'Swift apology, then let's get going!'

Quickly, she and Jack unclasped their seatbelts and rescued Twitchy, who was rolled up in a rug. Then Leonora clambered up the conning tower's ladder, pushed open the hatch and prepared to face the music.

It's safe to say she wasn't prepared for the scene that awaited her. Because instead of any music-facing (or tellings-off so colossal she could have heard them from space) there was . . . total silence.

All the villagers looked very strange. It was as if they'd been frozen in time, which, on closer inspection, they absolutely had. Their arms were raised, their faces contorted, but their eyes were glassy. Upturned tables and chairs hung in mid-air. Choux buns, sausage rolls and lemon drizzle cakes were suspended all round their heads, like some kind of freeze-frame food fight.

Leonora, quickly followed by Jack, scrambled out on to the top of the submarine, trying not to slip on the raspberry jam and caramel that smeared the hull. They managed to jump down on to the grass, blinking hard and rubbing their eyes. Because more surprising than any of that (which was all pretty gob-smackingly incredible), Leonora saw someone they hadn't been expecting to see there at all.

Standing right in the centre of the destruction, in her neat black suit, was Professor Prisha Puri from SIG.

7
Cupcake Massacre

'Professor Puri! Wh-what are you doing here?' stammered Leonora.

The professor was holding an umbrella-like object in one hand. It beamed complex colourful patterns on to the ceiling of the marquee. All the villagers were staring upwards at them as if mesmerized, shiny strings of drool escaping their slack jaws.

'Leonora, my dear girl, you're in supreme danger!' said Professor Puri.

'No kidding,' agreed Jack. 'She's just smooshed Brenda Spaniel's cupcakes.'

'How are you, Professor Puri – how does that *work*?' cried Leonora, momentarily forgetting the bit about supreme danger and gazing in astonishment at the umbrella.

'It's a Temporal Interrupter Module. It disrupts local time, but only for a few minutes. Listen. Your uncle has escaped from Crabby Island. He'll be here any moment. You must all leave this instant!'

Leonora felt her stomach drop ten floors.

'But how did he – how did he find me?'

'Gosh, I think I can explain that.' A sturdy-looking man standing beside Professor Puri stepped forward. He had a kindly face and the most magnificently chaotic eyebrows she had ever seen. 'We believe your uncle must have read the local news reports about Jack's recent return home to Snorebury. He must have guessed you'd still be together.' The man shook Leonora warmly by the hand. 'My dear, I often hoped we'd meet. I'm Professor Echo.'

'Huh?' Leonora blurted out. 'But – but aren't you a missing person?'

'Goodness, is that what they're reporting? No, I'm *on the run*. Luther's chums in the police are awfully keen to apprehend me.'

'Well, blow me down! Kenneth!' cried Mildred, as she emerged from the submarine with Captain Spang following behind. 'Can it be you?' She slid inelegantly down the slick hull and landed with a great **FROMPH** on the grass. As she brushed herself off, she and Professor Echo exchanged surprised looks and then embraced.

'My dear Professor Dribble!' he cried. 'Goodness me, it's wonderful to see you again. But we can't talk for long – you're not safe here. Luther is on his way, and there's a spy in the society. We believe our leader, Professor Insignia, has betrayed us all. He's been

working with Luther.'

'No way!' said Jack, his eyes like dinner plates.

'I'm afraid so, my boy. It looks as though Insignia has given Luther access to his emotion formula,' Professor Echo continued, 'and Luther needs to be jolly well stopped!'

Leonora tried to clear her head, but it felt like a shaken snow globe with all the many questions she had swirling around. So her uncle had finally got his greedy hands on Insignia's emotion formula – but what was it? Leonora guessed it was some kind of method to copy human feelings. And she *did* know that her uncle would use it for terrible purposes.

'Look,' she said, rummaging in her pocket for her graph. 'Twitchy's been picking up vibrations. I think they're coming from the deep ocean, where I think Mum and Dad are hidden.'

Professor Puri took the crumpled piece of paper and studied the readings. Then she and Professor Echo looked at each other, both of them worried.

'These tremors are new,' said Professor Puri. 'They're stronger than the ones our surveillance teams have reported. We'll need you to go and investigate at once.'

'Why us?' said Jack, alarmed.

'The society has been compromised,' said

Professor Puri. 'There could be other spies in SIG. And we *can't* let Insignia or Luther know we're on to them.'

'Och, how long before Luther arrives?' asked Captain Spang.

'Gosh, let's see –' Professor Echo checked his watch – 'maybe ten minutes, eleven if we're lucky?'

Just then, they heard the screech of car tyres from outside the marquee. A shiny golden Rolls-Royce appeared at the top of the high street. It rumbled downhill and came to a stop outside the shops only a hundred metres away. Leonora gasped, then watched in dread, as the door

opened and out stepped – Uncle Luther.

He looked even scrawnier than usual, dressed in a black silk suit and white fur coat. His bony fingers glittered with jewelled rings. He grinned at his own image in the toyshop window before turning back towards the marquee. His glare froze Leonora like the north wind.

'Quickly, everyone – we've got to get out of here!' she cried, stumbling backwards. Behind her (and thankfully hidden from her uncle's line of sight) the submarine looked like a marooned whale at a toddler's birthday party. Professor Puri's Temporal Interrupter Module machine was starting to lose power and the patterns on the roof of the marquee were stuttering and fading. Time was starting again!

'We'll stall Luther, while you get away,' said Professor Echo, giving Leonora an affectionate nod. 'Go quickly – find out what's causing these readings!'

By now, all the villagers were starting to blink awake, their faces etched with confusion, as egg sandwiches and raffle tickets began to rain down. Uncle Luther was striding across the green, shoving small children aside.

Professor Echo clapped his hands together and cried, 'Well, gosh and goodness, just look! It's a special celebrity guest – Luther Brightspark!'

Everyone turned to gawp. There were excited gasps (and giggles, especially from the parish grannies). Then all at once, the good people (and downright awful people) of Snorebury rushed forward and mobbed Uncle

Luther. His face flushed with utter disgust at being so close to his adoring public.

'Quickly – now's our chance!' cried Leonora. She ran to the back of the submarine and pushed with all her might. Jack and Captain Spang helped too, but the *Aquabolt* was stuck fast.

'No, hang on,' wheezed Leonora, 'we need something to – to reduce the friction!' She stopped pushing and began grabbing handfuls of cake instead. She started to daub the sub's underside with buttercream icing, apple mousse, lemon curd – anything that came to hand.

Jack, looking seriously confused, helped too. Mildred,

meanwhile,
wrapped one end of a length of bunting round her middle and the other round the conning tower.

Then she heaved like a one-woman tug-of-war.

Slowly, but surely, the submarine started yielding to Mildred's great strength and the slippery custard. It began inching its way out of the back of the marquee. Mildred quickly unwrapped the bunting and went to the back to help Leonora and the others push.

All at once, the vessel gained momentum. It slipped away from them, off the grass and down the final stretch of road towards the slipway. Leonora felt a jab of satisfaction. It was poetry in motion (or Newton's Second Law of Motion in motion). The force of them all pushing, the greasy patisserie, the sub's aerodynamic form – everything worked in harmony to achieve perfect acceleration.

The only problem was – no one was inside.

8
Harbouring Fugitives

SPLOOOOOOOOORRRRSSSH!!!

Leonora, Jack, Twitchy, Mildred and Captain Spang, racing to the quayside, heard the sub smash headlong into the harbour's tranquil waters. For a few agonizing seconds it disappeared completely. Then it bobbed back up like a popped cork.

'Oh wow, it's still in one piece!' cried Leonora, inwardly high-fiving herself. 'Come on, we've got to get aboard!'

She glanced back over her shoulder towards the fete. Her uncle was completely hidden in a huge crowd – for now. She waved the others along the harbour wall to where the sub was now floating a few metres below them.

'Look – there's a ladder,' said Jack.

'I can't get down that. My poor knees!' cried Mildred.

'Please, Millie, we're not going anywhere without you,' said Leonora, pretending she hadn't noticed the ladder's rusty rungs. 'It's OK, I'll go first.'

Leonora lifted Twitchy into her rucksack and hoisted him over her shoulders. She clambered down the ladder, landing on top of the submarine. It pitched and rolled. She slipped on butterscotch but somehow managed to cling on, wriggling up the conning tower and down into the vessel.

Inside it was very dark. Leonora scrabbled around and picked up her ultraviolet diver's light, thinking it was a normal torch. When she switched it on, she saw something she

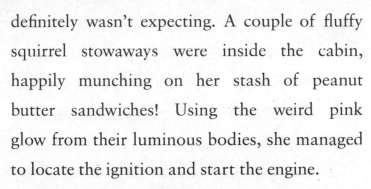

definitely wasn't expecting. A couple of fluffy squirrel stowaways were inside the cabin, happily munching on her stash of peanut butter sandwiches! Using the weird pink glow from their luminous bodies, she managed to locate the ignition and start the engine.

The propeller whirred, the water churned and bubbled, and there was a waft of diesel as Leonora reversed nearer to the wall. One by one, the others managed to slip-slide across the deck, hurry through the hatch and make it down into the submarine. Mildred arrived last, squeezing herself inside and slamming the hatch shut with her spare hand.

'We did it! That was so close!' cried Jack, as they all flopped on to the benches and caught their breath.

'Far too close,' said Mildred, huffing. 'I never wants to set eyes on that man again!'

'Me neither,' said Leonora. 'Hold on!' She

turned a series of valves, adjusting the air pressure in the main ballast tanks to reduce their buoyancy (or, to use a *slightly* less technical term, their 'floatiness'). Slowly but steadily, the submarine began to sink.

Leonora breathed a huge sigh of relief as she heard the **SWASH** of seawater closing in above their heads. The cabin slowly grew cooler. She revved the engines and carefully steered them out of the mouth of the harbour. Away from Snorebury. Away from the fete-worse-than-death. Away from Uncle Luther.

'Is everyone OK?' she said at last. She glanced behind her and saw Mildred putting a copper kettle on the hob, Captain Spang and

Jack plumping bolsters, Twitchy reclining in his otter hammock.

'Aye, we're as right as we'll ever be,' said Captain Spang.

'OK! Then I'll set our course.' Leonora tapped the coordinates she knew off by heart into the control panel. Outside the now-clean viewport, everything looked peaceful and dreamlike. Shafts of sunlight slanted sideways down through the aquamarine water and shoals of little fish flitted this way and that.

'What do you think these read-outs mean?' Leonora said at last, rummaging in her pocket

for the graph and passing it to Mildred.

'I don't rightly know, sweetheart,' said Mildred after she'd puzzled over them a while. 'They're patterns of some sort. Almost like a heartbeat. I can't believes what Professor Echo told us though – my old boss Insignia . . . working *with Luther*?'

They all exchanged stunned glances. Leonora bit her lip. She couldn't believe it either, but then she remembered that her uncle had *been invited* by SIG to attend their meeting at Dyrne College, and it was *Professor Insignia* who had given him a warm welcome there . . .

'Maybe it was Insignia's plan all along,' she said, 'to give Uncle Luther access to the emotion formula. But what are the two of them going to do with it?' She knew she *had* to stop them.

'This Echo guy . . . you sure you can trust him?' said Jack.

Mildred sighed. 'Kenneth's a kind and

brilliant man,' she said. 'He adored teaching Eliza. And we *know* we can trust Prisha . . .'

'And remember – you were wrong about *certain people* last time?' Leonora whispered. She felt a stab of shame remembering how Jack had made her doubt Mildred's loyalty on their last adventure. Jack looked sheepish.

'Aye, well, these are some sorta sonic readings,' said Captain Spang, taking the paper from Mildred. He stroked his beard, his bangles jangling on his wrists. 'Mystical frequencies from a powerful underwater presence. Could be the Sea People's Choir . . . from the lost city of Atlantis!'

'The *what*?' chorused Leonora and Jack.

'You bairns might not believe it, but there are ancient tales of deep-sea music. When I joined the Azerbaijani Underwater Bagpipe Troupe – back in '82 it would have been – our conductor *swore* he'd heard underwater singing.'

Mildred snorted into her teacup. 'What are you flaffing on about, Angus? We need to concentrate. What are Insignia and Luther planning?'

'I don't know,' said Leonora. 'But I'm *sure* these vibrations are coming from the place he's hiding Mum and Dad in. It's approximately 756.32 nautical miles away and we're travelling at a speed of –' she tapped a dial – 'twenty knots, so . . . oh no, it's going to take us nearly two days!'

'What about when we gets there, sweetheart?' asked Mildred. 'We don't know what we'll find . . . and Luther's *dangerous*.'

'Yeah, last time you faced him, Leo, you had the Switcheroo,' said Jack. 'We can't turn up empty-handed. We need, like, super-cool weapons.'

'We do?' said Mildred.

'Stingray stun guns, double-barrel sand

cannons,' said Jack, counting the items on his fingers, 'jellyfish tasers with stings so sore even weeing on them won't help . . .'

'Oh, I forgot I told you about those,' said Leonora. 'Don't have any with me though.' She sighed and looked about the sub, realizing with a jolt that they were sailing into the unknown, unarmed (unless they could fend off mortal danger with scatter cushions). How long could Professor Echo and Professor Puri stall her uncle? How long before he came chasing after them?

'We could take a wee pitstop?' suggested Captain Spang.

'I don't need to go,' said Jack.

'Och no, I mean Crabby Island can't be far from here. We could get supplies there, eh?'

Leonora glanced at the Captain, feeling the tightness in her shoulders relax a little. 'You're right!' she said. 'The island *is* on our way. I made some gadgets for an escape mission a long while back. Stashed them in Crux Cove so my uncle wouldn't find them.'

'What *kind* of gadgets?' Jack asked. 'Invisible laser torpedoes?' He looked excited.

'Hmm, not *exactly*,' said Leonora, 'but they'll definitely help us.'

Jack flashed his lopsided grin. Mildred and Captain Spang nodded. Twitchy thudded his tail and gave her an approving squark.

'OK, that's settled,' said Leonora. She turned back to the control panel and tapped the new coordinates into the navigation screen. Their course was set for a small detour . . .

Home.

9
X Doesn't Mark the Spot

'You *sure* you buried whatever it is here?' said Jack, frowning.

It was midday, and Leonora and Jack were digging in the chilly, wet sands of Crux Cove. The beach around them looked as though a team of moles had gone totally berserk.

'Yeah, keep going. I know it's here . . . *somewhere.*'

Leonora shucked her spade into the sand, feeling a swell of happiness at being back on Crabby Island. If she stood on her tippiest tiptoes, she could just glimpse the glass dome of the lighthouse beyond those black cliffs. Part of her wanted more than anything to run up there to her beloved workshop, lock the door and never face the world again. But a much bigger part of her knew they couldn't stay long – not if she wanted to get her family back.

'Whoa – found something!' said Jack, moments later, his shovel making a loud **DINK**. He and Twitchy scrabbled in the sand and found a battered flight case. They hauled it out of the hole.

'That's the one!' said Leonora, leaning over the box. She undid the clasps and opened the lid to reveal . . . a set of small plastic cones. Leonora grinned. Jack looked unimpressed.

'They're nano-thrusters,' she said, holding

them up to the light. 'I was building a kayak made from kelp a while back . . .'

'O-kaaay . . .'

'With oars made from Mildred's reinforced crab spaghetti . . .'

'Makes total sense.'

'I was going to use these to make the kayak faster, but I got side-tracked building something else. Hope the mechanisms haven't seized up.'

Leonora inspected each of the cones before carefully replacing them. She then removed some other objects from a hidden compartment at the bottom of the box: oval-shaped masks and little green balls.

'No way. We haven't got time for snorkelling,' said Jack, eyeing the masks.

'No – they're oxygen masks. They enable you to breathe for up to twenty minutes underwater without tanks. And these are seaweed smoke bombs. They might come in handy.'

'Yeah, all right. Pretty useful,' he conceded. 'We'd better get going!'

Leonora nodded and replaced all the gadgets, snapping the case shut. She shoved it under her left arm while Twitchy jumped up and tucked himself under her right. Together they headed back to the submarine, which was moored in the cove behind them. The water was so icy it made their legs tingle. Mildred leaned over the side and pulled them up out of the cold.

Over the next hour, Jack helped Leonora stick the thrusters to each side of the hull. When they'd finished, she stood still for a few moments on deck, taking one last look back at her island. Her eyes started stinging and her throat tightened.

'You know, I – I think I need to get some spare wrenches from my workshop.'

'There's no time, Leo,' said Jack, gently tugging her arm. 'We've really got to go.'

Leonora hesitated, blinked back hot tears. Turning away at last, she motioned to Jack and together they headed inside.

Below deck, everyone started preparing for the journey ahead. Jack pulled down the periscope. Mildred secured the hatch. Captain Spang switched on the squirrels and fed them more peanut butter sandwiches. And Leonora tested the engine's new turbo power. Finally, she let air out of the ballast tanks to start their descent.

Slowly, steadily, they sank below the waves once more, navigating away from Crabby Island and into the deep blue. The light quickly faded.

Outside they could see the black fingers of eerie kelp forests, shoals of silver fish flashing like daggers. And there was an insistent pinging noise from the transducer (the sub's location system) bouncing off underwater objects.

'Guess we've got some time to kill. Anyone fancy a game?' said Captain Spang. He began dealing a pack of gilt-edged playing cards on to the table. Leonora turned on the cruise control and clambered into the main cabin to join him. 'Won these cards in Cairo a few years ago,' he said, giving her and Jack a mysterious wink. 'They've always brought me luck.'

Leonora smiled and turned over her hand. She held the Three of Tulips, the Six of Twigs, the Queen of Blackberries and the Ace of Spoons. She side-eyed Jack, who was failing to control a monstrous fit of giggles.

'You can deal me in too,' said Mildred, who'd been busy emptying the gruesome contents of her apron pockets into paper bags. 'I've broughts some travel sweets.' She beamed, passing around samples. 'Don't be shy – get stuck in!'

'Hmm . . . what flavours?' asked Jack.

'All the classics,' said Mildred. 'I've gots rhubarb and mustard, blobstoppers, swine gums, strawberry plaices, chocolate muttons, banana spits . . .'

'Och, delicious!' said Captain Spang, cheerfully helping himself to a fat black string of pilchard liquorice. (They say that love is blind. They never mention it has no taste buds.)

'You know what? I think I'll pass,' said Jack, pulling a face.

'Me too,' said Leonora, shooting Jack a knowing look. 'Anyway, I think we'd better check our course.'

Leonora and Jack left Mildred and the Captain to their cards and climbed back into the front seats. They gazed out of the viewport.

Leonora flicked on the external floodlights and a white beam radiated ahead of them, illuminating a few metres of the black ocean beyond. Before long they could see an unworldly array of marine life swirling all around. Luminous jellyfish and cuttlefish **SCHLOOPED** past. Grey swordfish bolted out of the darkness. It was dreamlike.

'Here – found this in one of my wildlife magazines,' said Jack. He pushed a glossy leaflet into Leonora's hand. It was an article from *National Subaquatic*.

FREE FISHADVISOR

Tourist Guide to the Deep/Deadly Ocean

SUNLIGHT ZONE

(surface-200 metres)

Enjoy the ocean's exclusive top tiers with stunning marine life, including sharks, dolphins, turtles - far too many species to mention! It never disappoints.

Traveller rating: Excellent.

TWILIGHT ZONE

(200–1,000 metres)

Discover a world of weird and bioluminescent (glowing) sea life, like lantern fish and giant squid. Unless you love plankton, lunch options are limited. So bring a picnic and make a day of it.

Traveller rating: Good.

MIDNIGHT ZONE

(1,000–3,695 metres)

Looking to avoid the crowds? This zone is for you. Plus, the hydrothermal vents are a bit like mineral spa baths (if you don't mind water heated to 400°C).

Traveller rating: Good.

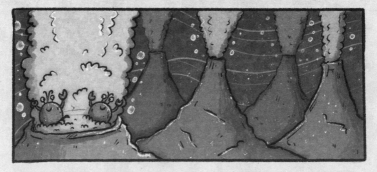

ABYSSAL ZONE
(3,695-6,000 metres)

They don't call it staring into the abyss for nothing. Down here the water pressure is extreme and there's no light or oxygen. Even worse, there's no Wi-Fi.

Traveller rating: Abysmal.

THE TRENCHES
(6,000-10,792 metres)

This is the deepest a manned submarine has ever gone. Not much wildlife, but plenty of free parking. (A sighting of a megalodon shark is not guaranteed.)

Traveller rating: Good.

NB FishAdvisor™ accepts no responsibility for holidays undertaken using this guide. Only a fraction of the deep ocean has been mapped, so we just totally made up the rest. Non-refundable, non-negotiable, non-helpful.

'Brilliant – thanks, Jack,' said Leonora, sticking the magazine cutting to the control panel. He grinned and they both settled back into their seats.

The minutes ticked over, and the hours raced after them. Thanks to the new thrusters, they were making good time. Leonora calculated that at this speed they'd reach the coordinates by early tomorrow morning. Everything was going *exactly* to plan. Nothing would stop her now.

Twitchy hopped up and curled himself into a furry otter ball on her lap. Leonora rubbed the back of her neck and yawned. In the lull of the cabin, all warm and secure, Leonora felt her eyelids grow heavy . . .

And before you could say 'Titanic', she'd fallen fast asleep.

10
Shipwreck Superhighway

TER-R-R-RINNNNG!!!

Leonora was booted from soothing sleep into the realms of the very wide awake. An ear-splitting alarm reverberated around the cabin, making her leap right out of her seat. The sub's warning lights switched on, bathing everything in a murderous red glow.

'Huh? What the – oh no!'

Leonora stared in horror at the completely blank navigation panel before her. She jabbed the screen. 'Oh, this is *so* not good!' she murmured, inwardly cursing her over-optimism. Maybe two car satnavs spliced with half a laptop *couldn't* navigate the deep ocean after all. Had it been an idiotic idea?

'Huh, Leo, what's going on?' mumbled Jack, groggily.

'Aye, is it morning?' Captain Spang and Mildred had woken bolt upright at the table, eyes wild, a few playing cards stuck to their flushed cheeks.

'Engine and thrusters are working fine, oxygen levels are OK, cabin temperature's stable. I just . . . I can't pin down our *exact* location,' reported Leonora. Her fingers flitted over the keyboard, typing commands. She tried to ignore the panic clutching her chest. They were three hundred metres below the surface and sailing blind, at the mercy of the wild ocean. How could she have been so stupid? She'd messed everything up. Their whole mission was in jeopardy!

'I'm sure you can fix this,' said Jack, passing

Leonora her rucksack. 'We'll help.'

'Yes, sweetheart, tell us what to do,' said Mildred.

Leonora took a deep breath and squinted through the viewport. The sub's floodlights pierced the gloom just enough for her to see that they were gliding above an oceanic shelf. There was a sandy seabed only a few metres below them.

'OK. We can cruise at this depth while I repair the navigator,' she said, starting to unscrew the device's main screen.

'Have you tried turning it off and on again?' said Jack, watching as she heated a soldering iron to fix the broken circuits. Before Leonora could answer this super-helpful suggestion, Captain Spang gave a sudden shout –

'Och, lassie – watch out!'

A huge ghostly form had appeared out of the darkness straight ahead of them. Leonora

dropped her tools and grabbed the steering levers just in the nick of time. She swerved hard, narrowly avoiding a . . . *shipwreck*. They sailed past the scuttled vessel lying on its side in the sand. It was covered in cold-water corals, barnacles and crabs. Grinning eels leered from its broken hull.

Captain Spang jumped up, brushing a Seven of Twigs from his forehead. Then he pushed his way forward. 'I dinnae believe it!' he cried. 'It's – it's *Aboat Time*!'

'About time for what?' said Jack.

'No! *Aboat Time*. My old ship. One of the first ones I ever sank!' he cried, pressing his nose up against the viewport. He had a nostalgic look in his eyes.

'You sailed *that*?' said Leonora, staring at the forlorn wreckage.

'Aye, she was a beauty! Took her on some real adventures . . . until we had to be rescued when it sank. I think the Bavarian Navy came for us that time,' he said, stroking his beard.

'O-kaaay . . . so if we're near your old sailing routes, can you help navigate?' asked Jack.

Leonora frowned. On the one hand, Captain Spang *had* helped them locate Mavenbridge on their last adventure, but, on the other, she also recalled several near-death sailing experiences with him at the helm of his ferry. He could probably even get lost trying to exit his own cardigan . . . But she shook those doubts away. Right now, she needed all the help she could get.

'Thanks, Captain Spang,' she said. 'That would be great.'

Just then, Twitchy started pawing at her feet. He was letting out a complicated series of *neep*s and staring up at her with determination. His whiskers were vibrating at several times their normal speed.

'What's up, Twitch?' Leonora asked, bending down and rubbing her nose against his. 'Oh, I think he's picking up those deep-water vibrations again,' she said. 'Maybe you can help guide us too, Twitch.'

'Well, we'd better hurry up cos I think there's a leak!' cried Jack.

Sure enough, a thin trickle of liquid was pooling in the footwell.

'Oh no, it's the pressure!' gasped Leonora.

Her insides lurched. Her heart thudded in her chest. 'Some of the welding's coming undone!'

'Don't you be worrying, sweetheart,' said Mildred. 'You just focus on getting us to them coordinates. Jack and I will repair this damage.'

Mildred rooted through her grisly apron pockets and pulled out several sticks of Fishy-Fresh Chewing Gum™ (it had been Uncle Luther's favourite, which might explain why his breath could explode a goblin at fifty paces). She handed the repulsive green sticks to Jack, who stuffed them into his mouth and started chewing.

'Urggh! That's like school dinners times ten thousand!' he groaned, spitting a wodge of putrid gum into his hand.

'It's not that bad,' Mildred said, bristling. 'Just keep chewing and plugging them holes!'

Over the next few hours, Jack and Mildred stuck the fish-flavoured gum into the tiny cracks

that were appearing in the hull. When it ran
out, they used Mildred's infamous trout toffees.
Meanwhile, Leonora plotted their course via
Twitchy's seismic whiskers and a selection of
Captain Spang's maritime catastrophes that
littered the seabed: *Seas the Day* (rescued by
the Moldavian Offshore Unicycle Club), *Buoy*

Oh Buoy (the Swiss Synchronized Swan Pedalo team), *Pier Pressure* (the Zambian Extreme Aqua-Zumba Academy) and *Knot-at-all Shore* (the Girl Guides). On they went, following the shipwrecked boats along the seabed like they were characters in a strange aquatic retelling of Hansel and Gretel following the breadcrumbs.

In the grip of the mighty ocean, time seemed to shift and flex. While Leonora battled to fix the navigation panel, the little submarine nosed its way onwards, through deep-sea canyons, along ridges and over endlessly sandy plateaus. Until – at last –

'Ha, I've fixed it!' Leonora cried.

Barely a moment later, they reached the edge of another vast rock shelf. The seabed suddenly dropped away entirely and they found themselves floating above a black void.

'I – I don't get it,' Leonora said. She rubbed her eyes and peered out in confusion. 'We've made it — these are the exact coordinates,' she said, checking the now-behaving satnav, 'but there's — there's just nothing here.'

They all exchanged anxious looks and stared through the viewport. Leonora steered the submarine in a wide circle, desperately scouring the sea all around them. She wasn't sure what she'd been expecting, but maybe *some* signs of human life. All she could see, though, was a marine wilderness as empty as her aching heart.

'Mum?' she whispered. 'Dad? Where *are* you?'

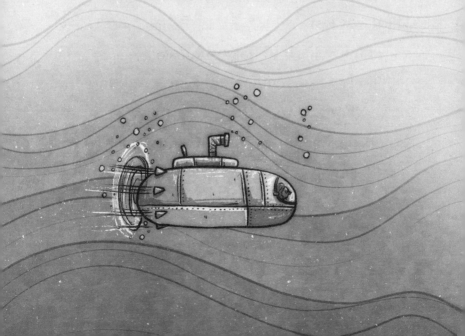

11
Sea-Life Disco

'Sorry, lass,' said Captain Spang, giving a weary shrug. 'Thought we were in the right place. This old seadog's been chasing his tail.'

'No, you've done a great job,' said Leonora, trying not to sound too colossally surprised. 'This is the correct longitude and latitude.' Then she double-checked the read-outs on the paper in her pocket against Twitchy's vibrating whiskers. 'And you've done brilliantly too, Twitch,' she said. He gave a proud little squark.

Leonora kept circling the little submarine, peering out in frustration. She ascended to twenty metres to search nearer the surface. The ocean slowly changed to a lighter, sapphire blue. Their ears popped like bubble wrap. But other than the odd frond of seaweed swirling around them, they couldn't see anything else. Leonora felt her hopes and dreams capsizing. All she could see around her was a vast watery void – a dead end.

'Uncle Luther, he's – he must have played a horrible trick,' she cried, bashing her fists on the control panel. Tears streamed down her grimy cheeks.

'It looks that way,' said Mildred with a sigh. 'That despicable man.'

Twitchy hopped up beside Leonora and nuzzled her neck. Everyone was quiet for a very long time. Only the mechanical whir of the engines filled the expanding silence.

Then at last Jack said, 'Um, Leo, the sea life . . . don't you think it looks a bit . . . *odd*?'

'What d'you mean?' She wiped her eyes. Looked up.

'Well, I've watched loads of wildlife programmes . . . and I've never seen fish do *that*.'

'Do what?' Leonora followed Jack's gaze downwards and, yes, something incredibly strange was happening in the darker water just a few metres below them. 'Oh . . . *wow*.'

Dozens of different species of fish were coming together in a giant silvery cluster. When little fish do this, it's called a bait ball, except this one looked more like a disco glitter ball. If Leonora didn't know better, she could have sworn she saw clownfish clowning around, conger eels doing the conga, dabs dabbing and squid giggling.

She pressed her palms to her eyes. Shook her head. *I'm tired. I'm seeing things. None of this is real*, she told herself. But when she looked up again, the jellyfish were joining in too – pulsing and twinkling, their beautiful bioluminescence shining all the colours of the rainbow.

'That's just so . . . weird,' said Jack. 'They look so . . . *happy*! What do you think's causing it?'

'No idea,' said Leonora. 'I've read about nitrogen narcosis. When divers go too deep it makes them act a bit loopy. But that's humans, not fish.'

'Aye, a few too many nips of fizzy pop, maybe,' said Captain Spang. 'They look as happy as clams at high tide.'

'Whatever it is, we'll need to go down to investigate,' said Leonora.

'But the leaks . . .' Jack frowned. 'And the crush depth . . . We'll get flattened like pancakes.'

'It's OK, we've got the submersible!' Leonora said, suddenly remembering the scooter. 'That can go much deeper.'

Quickly, Leonora made her way to the submarine's tail, re-opening the steel door. They all stared at the Shooter-Scooter 6.0 behind. Looks of admiration flickered across the faces of Mildred and Angus. Jack frowned again, although not quite as much as the first time he'd seen the homemade submersible.

Leonora felt her stomach twist.

Would the scooter be able to cope with the immense pressure outside? Or was it about to be Pancake Day, just like Jack said?

'I'm going to launch the scooter,' she said, as calmly as she could manage. 'We might have got to the right longitude and latitude but not the right depth. I'll see what's happening down there.'

'Do you have to?' said Jack. 'Can't we just hang here and see what happens?' There was a faint creak of metal, then a **FLOOOOSSH** as the sub sprang another leak. Leonora calculated they could only stay submerged for a maximum of eleven minutes, twenty-eight seconds –

'No, we can't. But it's OK. I can go on my own.'

'You will *not*!' cried Mildred. 'I'm coming with you!' They all eyed the tiny submersible, then looked back at Mildred. There was an uncomfortable pause.

'No, I'll go,' said Jack. 'I reckon I can fit in there. But what if it's – what if it's even more dangerous the deeper we go?'

Leonora reached for her rucksack. Inside was an assortment of screwdrivers, a shark-headed hammer, the seaweed smoke bombs and the oxygen masks.

'It'll be fine,' she said. 'We'll improvise. Millie, Captain . . . we've got to split up. It's not safe for the sub to stay under. You've got just enough fuel to go back the way we came, but you'll have to stay near the surface. Get a message to Professor Puri and Professor Echo. Ask them to send help!'

'No, I'm not leaving you here, sweetheart,' Mildred said, just as the lighting system started flickering on and off.

'Och, Millie, come on now. Leonora's right,' said Captain Spang, gently. 'It's not safe. We need to turn round, get some sorta back-up.'

'It'll be OK, Millie,' said Leonora. 'Ascend and sail back to Crabby Island along the surface. Call for help. We'll meet you back there.'

Mildred's brow furrowed. Her eyes filled up. Leonora hurried into her arms. At that moment it felt like the only safe place in the world.

'I don't likes this one bit,' Mildred said softly, stroking Leonora's hair.

'I know, but it's the only way. I'll be careful, I promise,' Leonora whispered back.

The red cabin lights flickered again. There was another urgent **TRIIING** noise from the control panel.

'Come on, we've got to get out of here,' said Leonora. Mildred wiped her eyes and let her go.

Over the next few minutes, Leonora explained the sub's controls to Captain Spang. Then she, Jack and Twitchy clambered inside the tiny submersible, pulling the round Perspex hatch down and screwing it shut.

As they prepared for launch, Leonora fought back tears. Would Mildred and the Captain make it back to safety? Would *they* make it back to safety? She felt Jack's warm hand squeeze her shoulder. Her fear eased a tiny fraction. She had to try. She *had* to see for herself what was in the depths.

Leonora looked up and signalled to Mildred and the Captain, who gave them one last anxious wave before closing the door. Almost at once, a valve opened above them. Seawater started gushing into the space around the scooter. A hatch in the floor of the *Aquabolt*'s tail then slid open beneath them. The scooter was launched out of the bottom and sank further down, down, down into the black abyss.

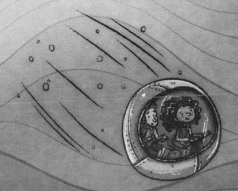

12
Into the Deep

For several minutes, Leonora fought to keep the scooter upright as it sank further into the dark waters. The *Aquabolt* became nothing but a faint shadow in the water far above their heads, before it disappeared completely.

'Whoa, this is awesome!' said Jack, fidgeting in the back seat. Twitchy squarked cheerfully as if they were taking a pleasure cruise, not exploring the treacherous depths.

'What are *you* so happy about, Twitch?' Leonora muttered as she revved the throttle. She could just make out the fast-disappearing glittery ball of fish below them and accelerated to catch up with it. When she glanced down to check their speed, something peculiar caught her eye. A large black plastic button protruded from the dashboard. It read:

CAMOUFLAGE

'Weird,' she murmured, brushing her fingertips over the button. 'I didn't put that there.'

'This is *so* fun!' gabbled Jack. 'How deep can we go again?'

'Really deep – 1,317.6 metres – although we'd have to be quick. The air supply is much less than the submarine. We'll have –' she checked her watch – 'two hours, thirty minutes and twenty-four seconds before it runs out.'

'Bags of time,' said Jack happily.

Leonora wished she shared his irritatingly sunny outlook. She could sense the water pressure building around them, as if they were being gripped by a mighty, watery fist. In fact,

Leonora calculated the pressure outside was now greater than an elephant standing on a postage stamp. And this thought (while scientifically fascinating) made her shudder with fear. Would her little Shooter-Scooter 6.0 survive?

They carried on slowly going down, down and down some more. It wasn't long before Leonora lost track of the fish. And all sense of direction too. That was because the deep ocean is darker than a black hole fitted with blackout blinds. The scooter's headlights only gave out a weak beam of light to guide them, and it became increasingly cold, the air smelling of old wetsuits.

'Should have brought some squirrels to light the way,' said Jack cheerfully.

'Yeah, that might have helped.' Leonora leaned forward and squinted into the murk. She made a mental note to design some ocean defoggers for the next voyage, or maybe some super-high-visibility eyeballs to mimic the spook fish drifting outside.

The minutes ticked by – then an hour. Leonora could feel her hopes sinking with the scooter. Could her parents really be down here in this abyss? They couldn't search much longer. Their air supply was running out. They would have to turn round soon . . . or they wouldn't get back at all.

But, beside her, Jack was behaving like he didn't have a care in the world. 'Don't you feel *brilliant*?' he said. 'Isn't this the best day of your life?'

'Jack, what's going on? First the happy fish, and now you and Twitch are extra happy . . . Snap out of it!' Leonora couldn't work out why he and Twitchy were behaving so strangely. She calculated it was nearly time to ascend back to the surface. And there was nothing here.

But just as Leonora was preparing to abandon

the search, she saw something in the water that made her do a double take. An enormous, curved structure suddenly appeared in the ocean ahead of them. It was the most astounding thing Leonora had seen in her whole life. It looked like a futuristic deep-sea chandelier, all glass and steel. Around the building floated bizarre-looking fish with see-through bodies and barrel eyes. Bright neon lights pierced the subaquatic gloom.

Jack gasped. Twitchy squeaked. Leonora felt like cool electricity was prickling every inch of her skin. She'd found it. *At last!* This was what Uncle Luther had been secretly working on all these years. It was beautiful, mesmerizing – utterly astonishing.

She took a deep breath and steered straight towards it.

13
Incredibly Lair-y

Leonora cut the scooter's engine and lights, but she still felt exposed as they drifted towards the strange structure. It didn't help that Jack was now laughing like a hyena on helium and Twitchy was wriggling about making playful *neeaab* sounds.

'Seriously, both of you, cut it out,' she whispered. 'We don't want to give ourselves away!'

'Whoa, what is this place? It's *epic*,' said Jack.

They gazed at the complex. It was

composed of a series of large pod-like interconnecting rooms. Curved glass-and-metal walkways snaked between them. It looked as if it had dropped into the ocean from outer space, as if NASA had mixed up its astronauts and aquanauts (an easy mistake to make).

As Leonora took it all in, she couldn't help but feel impressed. It was a spectacular feat of engineering. But what on earth (or under sea) was Uncle Luther creating that needed to be hidden *here* of all places? Was he inside? The thought made her tummy flip. She knew that Professor Echo and Professor Puri had promised to stall him. But for how long?

'We're sitting ducks here,' she said. 'Uncle Luther might see us. We need to hide ourselves, so there's nothing else for it.'

Leonora took a deep breath and pushed the mysterious camouflage button. There was a **SISSS**ing noise and the scooter's Perspex hatch seemed to suddenly steam up. They could still see out, but as they drifted past one of the huge pods Leonora couldn't see the scooter reflected in its glass. They seemed to have melted into the water, like fish using countershading* to hide from prey.

'I – I don't understand,' said Leonora, realizing they were now all but invisible in the water. Where had the button come from and what, exactly, had it done?

'No one can see us, so we need to break in. *Quickly*!' she said.

'What, like – like underwater burglars?' Jack burst into another fit of giggles.

'Right, that's it – you asked for it.' Leonora opened the glovebox and pulled out a tin of Awful Offal Travel Pastilles. As she clicked open the lid, a pungent aroma filled the air. Mildred

---

* More amazing animal science! Fish like tuna are darker on top and lighter on the bottom. This is called countershading and it makes them harder to spot.

had really outdone herself this time. It was as stinky as seven skunks in a sauna.

Leonora held a hand over her nose and fed Jack and Twitchy one of the pastilles each. Their jolly mood dispersed immediately.

'Bleuurgh, Leo, why did you do that?' Jack cried, gagging on the putrid sweet.

'Because I need you to *concentrate*,' she replied.

The change in Jack's mood was so sudden it made Leonora start to think. She realized that something she didn't yet understand must have been causing Jack's and Twitchy's cheerfulness. And it must have been the same thing affecting the sea life too. But a strange force that could overpower you and make you happy? It didn't make sense.

Just then, a timer on the dashboard started to **PING-PING-PING**. It meant their oxygen supply was critically low. Time was running out – they had to start their ascent!

Several thoughts wrestled inside Leonora at once. She just *had* to get inside this building to find out if her parents were there. And she *had* to stop whatever dreadful scheme Uncle Luther was plotting. But she was placing Jack, Twitchy – all of them – in the most terrible danger. Her thoughts bounced like a wrestler on the ropes for a moment, but then she came to her senses.

'This isn't the right thing to do. We'll have to resurface!'

'Leo, we're so close,' said Jack solemnly. 'Why don't we use the oxygen masks you brought from the island?'

'They only give us an extra twenty minutes of air. It's still too dangerous.' She restarted the engine and turned the scooter back round.

'But, Leo, you've brought us this far. We can't turn back now!'

Leonora faltered, glancing over her shoulder

at Jack's earnest expression. He was willing to take another huge risk to help her. Maybe the ultimate risk. An intense feeling of gratitude swelled inside her. She was certain she didn't deserve a friend as good as him.

'OK . . . if you're sure,' she said.

'Course I'm not sure. And you'll owe me *loads* of sweets. Proper ones.'

With that, Leonora shot Jack a nervous grin and pulled out the oxygen masks from her rucksack. They placed them over their faces and she circled the scooter back round again.

Closer and closer they drifted towards the ominous pods and, before long, they were sailing right underneath the complex. As Leonora manoeuvred them through colossal concrete legs rising from the seabed, she noticed that one of them had a small entrance built into it, a door that was sliding up and down very slowly.

'That's it, our way in,' she said. Leonora

edged the scooter closer and waited beside the door, timing the seconds between each slow opening. Then –

'Hold on!'

She revved the engine and accelerated hard. There was a strong gushing force as they swept under the closing door, and a clanking sound like bin lids being bashed together underwater. Then everything went dark.

'What the – where *are* we?' whispered Jack after several tense minutes.

'Not sure. Keep quiet.'

Leonora could feel that the pressure seemed to have given way. She calculated that the scooter was in an airlock, bobbing on the *surface* of the water.

'I think we might be in – I don't know – some kind of air-filtering system maybe?' Leonora pulled out her torch and flicked it on. They were floating inside a small concrete chamber, seawater lapping against the sides of the scooter. She cautiously popped open the hatch then lifted up her mask an inch, motioning for Jack and Twitchy to do the same. Cold air rushed around them.

As they gulped long slow breaths, Leonora realized she'd done it – she'd made it inside the complex! But her sense of relief disappeared in an instant, because what should they do now? The door they'd come through – their only escape route – was now firmly shut. They were trapped hundreds of metres below the ocean's surface. They were completely and utterly on their own. And who knew what was waiting for them in the eerily abandoned pods above?

And as if all that wasn't bad enough, they could suddenly hear the most dreadful, mournful sound echoing in the dark space all around them.

'**HELP!**' it said.

14
Echo Chamber

'What was that?' whispered Jack.

'I – I'm not sure,' said Leonora. 'Sounds like a woman's voice.'

Leonora aimed the torch beam above their heads. The noise seemed to be coming from some large metal vents fixed into the ceiling. 'Come on, we've got to follow that sound,' she said.

'Do we have to?' Jack had eyes like an owl on a rollercoaster.

'I'm afraid so. Quick as we can.'

Leonora bounced the light round the chamber to reveal a steel platform a few metres away.

They leaned over the sides of the scooter and paddled through the freezing water, bringing the vessel close enough for them to scramble out. Leonora helped Twitchy into her rucksack and hauled herself up on to the gangway. Then she turned, grabbed Jack's arm and pulled him up too.

'HEEEELP MEEEEEE!'

That awful cry again. Leonora's blood ran cold. *What if it's my mum?*

'There must be a way up into the main pods,' she said, her eyes darting wildly about her.

'How about through the vents?' suggested Jack, nodding upwards. 'Super-baddie lairs always have heating vents you can crawl through. That's just a fact.'

'We could. Or we could just use that door.' Leonora gestured towards a small rectangular entrance just to the left of them. Crouching down, she removed a hairgrip from her curls and made short work of the lock.

Twitchy let out a low, rumbling growl. Leonora tried to ignore the high-voltage panic now crackling through her veins. What would be waiting for them on the other side? What terrible plot had Uncle Luther and Professor Insignia been hatching all these years? She shook the thoughts away, clenched her fists and pushed open the door.

They found themselves inside a dark and windowless workroom. It had four rows of benches covered in curious contraptions. Leonora pointed the beam from the torch on to the labels, which she noticed were each embossed with a pale blue heart. They read the labels.

'What *is* this stuff?' whispered Jack.

BARBED-WIRE LOO ROLL ♡

STINGING-NETTLE ♡
NIGHT CREAM

SELF-POPPING ♡
BALLOONS

'No idea,' she whispered back. 'It's like a storeroom for – for bad prototypes or something. Come on.'

They crept towards the exit, then into a dimly lit curving glass corridor. Strange sea creatures floated serenely outside. They could hear the buzz of lights and smell a background whiff of disinfectant. The corridor sloped upwards, criss-crossing with other walkways, but there were no signs of people anywhere. It was totally deserted.

'Leo, I don't like this one bit,' whispered Jack.

'Me neither,' she said, her pulse galloping.

They instinctively crouched down,

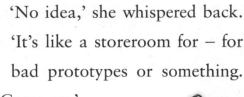

CONCRETE CUSHIONS

IMMORAL COMPASS

HOMEWORK MULTIPLIER

MISERY-GO-ROUND

133

backs against the walls. Leonora felt about as quiet and stealthy as a rhino in tap shoes.

They made their way upwards. All the time the cries for help kept getting louder and louder. At last they seemed to be nearing the centre of the complex, like the middle of an intricate spider's web. Curiosity was exploding inside Leonora's brain. Longing burned in her chest. There was no turning back. She needed to find out what was inside. To know the truth – even if it was terrible.

They finally arrived at a circular white door. It slid open.

'WHOA!' Leonora and Jack gasped together.

'SQUARK!' squarked Twitchy.

Before them was a cathedral-like glass chamber illuminated by dazzling lights. It was filled with dozens of scientists going about their work. They were wearing white laboratory coats with strange silver devices pinned to their chests.

All around the chamber, plasma screens blinked and bleeped with graphs, complex 3D diagrams and lines of computer code. Suspended high above them, in the very centre of the space, was what looked like a gigantic lightbulb inside a glass tube. It pulsed with menace.

Jack and Leonora grasped each other's hand and stood together, trembling and gazing all around them. Below the lightbulb they could see a podium on which a golden throne faced away from them. Slowly – smoothly – the throne turned round to reveal –

'Uncle Luther!'

Leonora's legs nearly buckled under her. Uncle Luther was sitting calmly, his smile set like an ambush.

'Well, well,' he sneered, bringing the rotating throne to a stop. 'There you are at last. My silly little *mess* – I mean *niece*. So good of you to drop in!'

He'd swapped his white fur coat for a laboratory coat. Leonora could smell cloying hair oil wafting off his greasy wig. She felt a wave of dismay as she noticed a familiar figure beside him making high-pitched wails into a microphone.

'Jolly good acoustics,' Professor Echo chuckled, glancing their way. 'I certainly sound like a damsel in distress, don't you think?'

'*Professor Echo!* How *could* you?' Leonora blurted out. 'My mum, Millie – they trusted you. We *all* trusted you!' To think that all this time Professor Echo had been the spy, not Professor Insignia!

He shrugged. 'Prisha was hard to shake off . . . but we outsmarted her. We knew we couldn't snatch you from under her nose in Snorebury. So we had to lure you here. She thinks Luther's still looking for you in Mavenbridge!'

'But why would you betray them?' said Jack.

'A man of my great intellect can't be expected to survive on the pittance the society pays me,' he said. He waddled off to sit at a sleek desk filled with computers, then stuffed a triple-cream doughnut into his mouth and carried on with his work, as if it was just another day at the office.

'What *is* this place?' Leonora's eyes darted around for any sign of her parents. Her voice was thick, words catching in her throat.

'This place is my life's work,' Uncle Luther said, momentarily closing his eyes as if lost in a delightful daydream. 'It's everything I've ever wanted.' Then his eyes snapped open again, as the door behind them slammed shut.

'And unless you do exactly as you're told, my little apprentice, it will be the last place you ever see.'

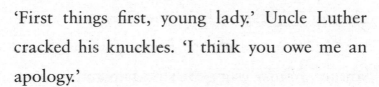

15

The Happiness Capacitor

'First things first, young lady.' Uncle Luther cracked his knuckles. 'I think you owe me an apology.'

'I owe *you* an apology?' Leonora felt a wave of outrage.

'For sending me back to that godforsaken island. Stopping me taking my *rightful* place at the society! Fortunately, Kenneth here has assisted me in obtaining Insignia's emotion formula. So I've finally been able to perfect *this*.' He gestured to the bulb pulsing in the air high above them.

'What *is* that thing?' said Jack, mesmerized.

Uncle Luther sneered. 'Ah, you again. The little nobody. Joel or Jimmy or whatever your name is. So many of you it's impossible to tell you apart.'

'H-how do you know about my family?'

'I make it my business to know. And *that*, my boy, is my happiness capacitor. The crowning glory of Brightspark Industries! It runs on a new kind of energy derived from pure joy. Everything you see around you –' he stood up and gave an expansive wave of the arm – 'is powered by human wonderment and delight!'

Leonora flinched. She couldn't think of a single human being less qualified to run the earth's happiness supply. She wouldn't trust her uncle to run a bath.

'And that's not all,' Uncle Luther continued, now striding up and down, clearly warming to his theme. 'This machine will amplify joyful human energy like electricity, use it to power cars, skyscrapers, cities – the whole planet! A boundless new energy supply which, naturally, I will control. I'll sell your own happiness back to you at a hundred times the price!'

His eyes gleamed like black ice. He looked as if he'd fallen out of the smug villain tree and hit every branch on the way

down. Leonora couldn't help but feel a tremor of awe mingled with her fear. As an inventor herself, she knew the happiness capacitor was quite an astonishing achievement.

'But how does it *work*?' she asked. She cringed to hear the interest in her own voice.

'Oh well, now, I can fill you in on that,' began Professor Echo. He tapped commands into his keyboard and a colourful graph appeared on a large screen behind him. It looked exactly like the strange readings Twitchy's whiskers had been picking up.

'Professor Insignia found that people emit emotions a bit like electromagnetic radiation. He also pioneered some extraordinary work into the *physical* properties of our emotions. It turns out anger is extremely heavy and dense. Envy is acidic. Pride is brittle. And did you know that sadness can be dissolved in water? A warm bath or hot cup of tea is perfect . . .'

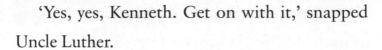

'Yes, yes, Kenneth. Get on with it,' snapped Uncle Luther.

'We refined the processes and focused our efforts on happiness, found we could harvest it from a distance without our subjects even knowing about it. So we set up receptors all around the world to pick up and store those happiness frequencies. Then we learned to amplify them – make them stronger. Of course, we've still got to get the unpleasant side effects ironed out . . .'

The graph spiked. The bulb burned brighter. Paper spooled out of a nearby machine. Professor Echo picked it up and examined the results.

'Let me see now . . . so a Miss Stephanie Ostrich in Vienna has just been handed a delicious cinnamon bun; the whole of Nigeria is enjoying a national holiday; the Argentinian men's needlework team has just won the Crochet World Cup; and, er, a Mr Bob Fnork in Bognor has been promoted – oh no, hang on, he's been promoted to headteacher, so that happiness will cancel itself out.'

'But why here?' Leonora persisted. 'Why so deep underwater?'

'It turns out happiness is magnetic,' said Uncle Luther. 'We tried building the machine on land, but we kept getting crowds of silly people turning up at the lab thinking it was their birthday or something. And we needed to avoid being detected by SIG. Down here, we're quite undisturbed.'

Leonora shuddered. So *that* was why Jack and Twitchy (and all the sea life) had been behaving so strangely. They'd 'caught' the happiness. And she realized, too, why the scientists were wearing silver boxes on their chests. Being close to the happiness capacitor could make you spectacularly joyous unless you had some kind of insulation against its effects. *Mildred's Awful Offal Travel Pastilles must have worked as insulation too*, thought Leonora, when she remembered how Jack and Twitchy's happy mood vanished when she gave them a sweet. Leonora wondered why *she* wasn't affected. But then it suddenly made sense. Pain clutched her heart.

'My parents!' she cried, pulling off her locket and holding up the photograph in accusation. 'Tell me where they are!'

Uncle Luther paused and smirked. 'Well, now, they've been a marvellous help getting the capacitor up and running, ever since I lured them on that fake Arctic trip all those years ago. They'd only work for me if I made them believe they'd see you again. But I dangled that carrot in front of them one too many times, it seems. I'm afraid they haven't got the brain power left to finish the job. So that's why I need . . . *you*.'

'Me? I thought I was "stupid",' Leonora

said, through gritted teeth. 'Can't one of your amazing scientists help you?'

'Oh, they've tried. Seems they're lacking certain skills . . . a depth of imagination. Naturally, *you*'ve learned that intelligence from me. So here's my offer: *join me*. Finish my wonderful machine! And in return for your services I'll give you what you've always wanted.'

He strode over to a nearby wall and pressed his palm against a scanner. A blind lifted to reveal an adjoining laboratory. Sitting together, taking it in turns to look at a computer screen, she saw –

'MUM! DAD!'

Leonora sprinted over to the window, pressed her face against the glass. They were so close! She could see her mother's thoughtful face, her father's calmness, his dark eyes just like hers. She could almost touch them – after all these years!

Leonora suddenly felt as though she was in a blissful freefall. As if someone had pushed her from a plane into a fresh patch of heaven. She let out a great cry of delight that sent the happiness capacitor whirring into overdrive.

What would it feel like to hug them? Where would they go? Where would they live? Crabby Island, obviously, with – with Millie and the Captain too! Her beautiful home would be complete at last. She imagined showing Mum and Dad her wondrous workshop, collecting shells on the beach, holding her mother's hand. She pictured the blissful sunsets, their arms wrapped round her. Captain Spang serenading them all . . . OK, maybe not that last one.

'I'll do it – I'll finish your machine!' Leonora cried, turning back to face her uncle as he slowly – *spitefully* – made the blind come down again.

'Marvellous!' declared Uncle Luther. 'I knew you'd see sense. I need you to adjust the processors your parents seem incapable of fixing. Then I need the capacitor joined to our international grid immediately. Accomplish that and I'll guarantee your happy family reunion!'

Leonora nodded. She'd never felt more certain of anything. Never felt happier in her whole life. She gave Jack a feverishly excited smile. Then allowed herself to be led away.

16
Missing Piece of the Puzzle

'Leo, you can't do this! That machine's *dangerous*,' said Jack out of the corner of his mouth. They were following Uncle Luther as he marched along a dark passageway leading off the main pod.

'No, really, it'll all be fine!' she said, giddily. Leonora felt like someone was pouring liquid sunshine through her body. Her thoughts were a mishmash of laughter and sparklers and glittery rainbows. She clasped the locket even tighter in her hand. Everything was going to be brilliant! There was definitely nothing to worry about.

If only Jack would stop spoiling the mood.

'But don't you remember the last time we agreed to help him?' said Jack, urgently. 'We accidentally gave him the real Switcheroo! He nearly got into SIG!'

'That won't happen this time.' Leonora quickened her pace to keep up with Uncle Luther.

'It will! You can't trust him,' said Jack, grabbing her arm. Leonora shook him off.

'You don't understand, Jack. You've *got* a family. I just want my mum and dad!'

Leonora side-eyed Jack as they hurried on. He looked miserable. Some of the gloss seemed to be rubbing off her happy feeling. As they finally arrived at the entrance to another pod, Uncle Luther leaned his forehead against a screen. There was a **THRUNNNG** noise as it scanned his eye. The door then swished open and they all made to go inside.

'Not so fast, Master Nobody,'

sneered Uncle Luther, barring Jack's way. 'You stay out here.'

Jack nudged Leonora, his eyes wide.

'Sorry – we need to do exactly as Uncle Luther wants,' she said, shrugging. Twitchy growled from inside the rucksack, but Leonora ignored them both. She turned and stepped inside the room. The door slammed shut behind her.

Leonora found herself inside a brightly lit laboratory. In the centre was a neat white bench filled with the tools and components needed to complete her uncle's machine. There were electronic resistors, power connectors, batteries, spools of copper wire and the mother of all motherboards to fix. In any other circumstances, this type of puzzle would be Leonora's idea of a wonderful birthday present, but this was no game. The stakes were too high. Get it wrong and her parents would be lost all over again. Get it right and . . .

Leonora slipped the locket back round her neck. She took off her rucksack and let a displeased Twitchy out before getting started. Her first task was checking and adjusting parts on the machine's central processing unit. Before long she turned her attention to the software, tapping lines of code into a laptop beside her. There were several computer bugs causing the system to crash, but one was particularly tricky to fix.

As she got lost in her work, Uncle Luther paced like a prison guard at the front of the room. He was simmering with the menace of fifty un-caffeinated headteachers. Twitchy, meanwhile, scrabbled at her feet as if to say, 'No, Leo, don't do it!'

'Do hurry up,' said Uncle Luther, checking his watch every few minutes. 'The capacitor needs connecting to the international network at once!'

'I'm going as fast as I can,' she said, her voice scratchy.

'Not fast enough. I want to secure my place in history *today*!'

Leonora carried on fixing the code. She measured currents, checked voltages, tested sockets one by one to make sure they worked. Everything was functioning correctly. Just a few more connections to test, then Uncle Luther would have his missing piece and she would have hers.

But now she couldn't ignore the fact that the giddy happiness she'd felt was wearing off. Nagging doubts crowded her mind.

'Um, Uncle,' she said, pausing at last and rubbing her forehead, 'Professor Echo said the capacitor has some side effects. What are they?'

'I don't have time for your irrelevant questions!'

'B-but surely a true *genius* like you wouldn't have made a mistake,' she said smoothly, trying to conceal that she was coming to her senses again.

Uncle Luther paused, flicked a speck of dust from his suit. 'Yes, well,' he said, 'once we've harvested the raw happiness, subjects do tend to have problems recreating it. The energy transfer leaves some people unable to feel joy again, but that's really not my problem.' He shrugged. 'In fact, it's rather a positive side effect. Happy people don't buy lots of things they don't need from Brightspark Industries. So, you see, sadness is terribly good for business.'

Leonora could feel her pulse quicken. The

air felt thick and soupy. The edges of her vision started to ripple like pixels on a broken screen.

'You know, Leonora,' he continued, shooting her a triumphant look, 'we're not so very different after all. We'll both do whatever it takes to get what we want, won't we?'

Leonora lowered her gaze, ran her trembling hands over the circuit board before her. She took a deep breath to steady herself and her thoughts suddenly came into sharp focus, like mist clearing from a mountaintop. She felt an unexpected sense of calm, knowing just what she had to do.

Her fingers could work faster now that her mind was completely clear. She tested the final lines of code, sealed the circuit board up and tightened the screws. She scraped back her chair and stood up.

'Uncle Luther,' she said, 'it's finished.'

17
Spanner in the Works

Back in the main pod, Leonora's eyes darted about searching for Jack. But he was nowhere to be seen. She felt sick, as though all her internal organs were playing musical chairs. She'd been horrible to Jack and now he was lost in the complex. But where?

Twitchy was tucked back inside her rucksack with his head on her shoulder. She could feel him bristling with anxiety. Outside, sea life swirled peacefully in the black ocean, unaware of what was about to happen.

Leonora watched as two assistants clad in protective suits and visors carried her circuit board up a gangplank, then along a metal walkway to the happiness capacitor suspended high above. It looked to her like something from the space programme. Only this time it would be one small step for a man, one giant leap in the dark for mankind.

'I've given you what you wanted,' she said, turning towards her uncle. 'Now you don't need me any more. Let me go to Mum and Dad!'

Above her, the scientists finished carefully inserting the electronic circuitry into the machine. They sealed the glass tube and signalled to Uncle Luther and Professor Echo below.

'How marvellous!' Uncle Luther shrieked. He jumped up from his golden throne and clapped his hands together with childish delight. 'Seven long years I've waited for this moment! Lord Luther Brightspark, the world's greatest inventor, will soon control human happiness and use it to power the whole planet! Now let's see if I can –' he paused briefly – '*feel something.*'

'We had a deal!' cried Leonora, clenching her fists. Everyone appeared to have forgotten about her. The scientists were all gathered round banks of computer screens, typing commands, monitoring sensors, analysing data. Uncle Luther, meanwhile, was sitting back in his throne, having wires attached to his torso. Leonora could see nerves jangling in his jaw and a look of desperation on his hollow face.

'Uncle Luther, our agreement!' she shouted, one last time.

He turned to her, but his expression was lost – faraway – *empty*. His wig was slipping sideways and sweat poured down his face.

Leonora couldn't wait a second longer. She *had* to get her parents out before Uncle Luther realized what she'd really done to his machine. In one swift movement, she pulled the shark-headed hammer from her rucksack and sprinted forward to the window where she'd glimpsed her parents. She smashed the hammer against the glass. Over and over she pounded, glassy shards splintering all around, until she could see right into the space behind it.

All that was there was a blank metal wall.

'Oh, your parents aren't *really* here,' Uncle Luther said, with a sneer. 'What you saw earlier was just a little film I made, a recording. I've got them working on some of my other projects, out in the desert!'

'No – you liar!' wailed Leonora.

'Awfully sorry – *not*. You'll understand. Parents are over-rated anyway. Mine certainly were,' he said with a grimace. 'Now, Kenneth, let's get on with it!'

Professor Echo looked up and strolled over to a giant lever in the centre of the room. An excited smile played upon his lips. He seized the lever in both hands and pushed it forward.

FRRRRRUUUMM-MM-MM-IIIIIIING!

All at once, huge tremors and vibrations filled the pod. A pulsing sound like a million heartbeats echoed all around. The happiness capacitor burned brighter than ever. A dazzling white light radiated down, flooding the chamber. They all had to squint and shield their eyes. The measuring instruments around them went into overdrive, needles whirring, lights flashing, computers bleeping.

'Is it working, Kenneth? Nothing's happening!' cried Uncle Luther. He waved over some more of the white-coated scientists, who set about readjusting the wires attached to his chest. 'More power, Kenneth! Push it to full capacity!' he screamed.

Professor Echo frowned, then pushed the lever as far forward as it would go. The thrumming noises grew even louder and the happiness

capacitor began sparking and fizzing.

'I can't – I can't feel anything!' shrieked Uncle Luther.

'You know, Uncle, you might feel happy if you just did the right thing for once!' cried Leonora, slowly backing away towards the door.

'Be quiet, you wretched child!' he ordered. 'You won't ruin things for me this time!'

'Won't I?' Leonora replied. She thought about the secret circuit she'd built into his machine to make it malfunction. 'You've always said I'm a "silly little mess". Well, I'll show you how much of a mess I can make!'

As Leonora said this, there was a sudden **KER-AAASH!** then a flash of lights like stars backfiring. The capacitor's glass cracked and exploded and the tube burst into flames! An immense shower of sparks shot out, raining down all around them.

'No – no – what have you done? My machine!'

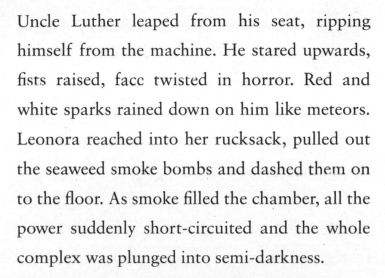

Uncle Luther leaped from his seat, ripping himself from the machine. He stared upwards, fists raised, face twisted in horror. Red and white sparks rained down on him like meteors. Leonora reached into her rucksack, pulled out the seaweed smoke bombs and dashed them on to the floor. As smoke filled the chamber, all the power suddenly short-circuited and the whole complex was plunged into semi-darkness.

'*Evacuate! Evacuate! All personnel to the escape penguins!*' announced a robotic voice from the tinny speakers all around. An emergency alarm began ringing in their ears. All the scientists were abandoning their desks, coughing and spluttering, stumbling for the exits.

'We've got to get out of here, Twitch!' cried Leonora. She crouched down and felt her way sideways towards the main entrance. It was hard to see anything in the smoke and chaos.

She heard screams and panicked footsteps. Leonora lit her torch just in time to dodge a huge shard of falling glass. Somehow, she made it back out into the corridor.

But only one thought hammered inside her head: *I have to find Jack!*

18
A Saviour in Tweed

Leonora stumbled along dark, winding corridors trying to find the laboratory where she'd last seen Jack. Her eyes streamed and her throat was choked with smoke. Terrifying tremors and explosions vibrated all around her.

As she ran, Leonora resisted the tidal wave of sadness trying to wash her away. She'd lost her parents . . . *again*. But she'd also broken Uncle Luther's diabolical machine and destroyed his schemes. Now all she had to do was find Jack. Where *was* he?

'**JACK! JAAAAACK!**' she cried. Her

voice was drowned beneath the screaming alarms. Twitchy squarked too with all his might, but there was no reply.

As they hurried on, Leonora could see a huge fire was now raging in the central pod. The structure started to warp and crack under the forces of heat and pressure. And then she noticed the dark waters outside were filling with something – penguin-shaped submersibles! All the scientists were evacuating and floating upwards to safety inside them, like rats deserting a sinking ship.

He must be this way! Leonora thought as she slid sideways through a closing door. But as she picked herself up and tried to get her bearings, her heart sank. She'd taken a wrong turn. She'd arrived at the launch bay *beneath* the complex. It was almost empty – all the escape penguins had gone. Something else caught her eye though, shimmering in the ocean about ten metres to her

right. Parked beneath the furthest launch bay, attached to the building above by its sunroof, stood the golden Rolls-Royce.

It looked so out of place there that Leonora half expected to see a subaquatic traffic warden too. She realized this could be their means of escape, only she *had* to find Jack – *now*!

'Come on, Twitch, let's go back,' she said, pulling off her rucksack and hauling him out. Twitchy stood up on his hind legs and fixed her with a steely look, as if to say, 'Yep, that's right. We're not leaving without him!'

They exchanged a brief hug and were about to retrace their steps when, to Leonora's horror, the main pod outside buckled and sheered away from the rest of the complex. It toppled on to the sandy seabed thirty metres away. There was another huge **KABOOOOM!** which knocked them both sideways, and they slapped on to the cold hard floor.

'**OOOF!**' cried Leonora.

'**SQUARK!**' cried Twitchy.

As she struggled to get up – limbs aching, heart thumping – Leonora heard something above the confusion that made her blood freeze in her veins. The tap-tap-tapping of a cane.

'Oh, you silly little mess. You're not going anywhere,' came the deep, rasping voice. Leonora spun round to find Uncle Luther stepping out of the smoke, right behind them. His white shirt was ripped open. His scrawny chest was covered with wires. His eyes were wild with uncontained rage –

'You've destroyed it! All of it!' he bellowed. 'I was so close – so close to my dreams!'

He towered above her, snarling. 'That machine was my life's work – my last hope!'

Leonora shrank away from him, shielding Twitchy behind her.

'I'll never work for you again!' she cried, her body trembling with terror. 'And neither will my parents. It's over!'

Uncle Luther paused, clenched his fist round his cane. 'Then I'll repay the favour. I'll keep you apart from them forever, do you hear me? *Forever*!'

'No, I'll find them in the end – no matter what!'

Uncle Luther flashed his wretched half-smile. Then, before she could duck out of the way, he grabbed Leonora's arm and twisted it.

'You're coming with me, *apprentice*. I'll never let you be free!'

His face was so close to Leonora's that she could smell his rank breath. A fat bead of sweat fell from his gaunt face and landed on hers. She felt fear tug every sinew, threatening to unravel her completely. She closed her eyes. Everything was exploding, collapsing around them. She couldn't break free. There was no way out. No escape this time.

But then the image of her parents flickered once more in her mind. *Never give up, Leonora,* she imagined them urging her. *Never give in!* And as she opened her eyes again, her heart did a cartwheel. She saw two small figures appear out of the darkness behind her uncle. Jack was sprinting towards her with someone else she definitely wasn't expecting to see. A rule-enforcer, a village-oppressor, a very unlikely saviour in tweed:

'Brenda Spaniel!'

'Stop right there, Luther!' Brenda boomed. She was wearing a tweed suit beneath her lab coat and ear defenders too. She dashed forward

with a clipboard and –

KAAA-WAAAALLLLOP!

Brenda slapped the board into the back of Uncle Luther's legs. He dropped to his knees, letting go of Leonora as he fell.

'Leonora – catch!' Brenda launched a sleek

metal tube into the air. Leonora only just managed to jump up and grasp the object. She knew at once what it was. Her Sonic Headteacher Demobilizer! Jack, meanwhile, performed an impressive football slide tackle and skidded to a halt beside her.

'You're all right!' cried Leonora as he got to his feet.

'Of course! Here – we need to use these.' Jack whipped out some jelly babies and shoved them into their ears. He then signalled to Leonora. She pulled out the demobilizer's metal pin, throwing it to the floor like a hand grenade.

SCREEEEEEEEEEEEEEEEEEEEEEEE!!

The device unleashed an incredibly high-pitched shrieking. It was a sonic force so brutal it could overwhelm humans – crush psyches – destroy entire civilizations! It was the amplified sound of Jack's siblings playing their violins together.

'EAAAARRRGGGHHH!!!'

Uncle Luther, who'd staggered to his feet, clamped his hands over his ears and doubled right over again, whimpering.

'Get out of here, all of you!' cried Brenda, motioning towards the Rolls-Royce.

'We can't leave you. Come with us!' cried Leonora.

'Don't worry. I have my own escape plans – go!' Brenda shouted, as another huge explosion ripped through the building. Water started gushing down the corridors. Uncle Luther jumped to his feet once more. He locked eyes with Leonora and gave her one last look of twisted fury. Then he fled the scene, with Brenda hot on his heels.

'Come on – let's go!' cried Jack.

They hurtled towards the loading bay, diving head first into the waiting car. Leonora and Twitchy scrambled into the front seat, while Jack slammed the sunroof shut. Leonora turned the keys and let the handbrake go, pushing all the pedals at once. The car lurched forwards. Then it slowly lifted up and away – away – away – into the ocean's deep embrace.

Leonora checked in the rear-view mirror and saw the great glass lair finally collapsing behind them. All the lights went out. She changed gears and slammed her foot down on the accelerator.

She had done it. She had stopped him. They were free.

19
Land Ahoy!

Leonora couldn't remember ever seeing such a welcome dawn. They'd spent anxious hours in the ocean depths until she'd calculated it was safe to surface. The Rolls-Royce burst through sunlit waves. Bands of crimson striped the horizon. They breathed cool, briny air.

'D'you think he's following us?' asked Jack.

'I – I don't know.'

Leonora scanned the ocean all around, but they were alone. There were no scientists, no penguins – and no Uncle Luther. In fact, there was nothing to suggest Leonora hadn't dreamed the whole thing.

'What *happened* back there?' said Jack, eyeing her curiously. 'How come you were acting so weird?'

Leonora touched her locket. 'The happiness was so strong, but the magnetic clasp on my locket must have repelled it . . . until I took it off.'

'But how did you smash everything up?'

'I saw that my parents had put a bug in the software to stop it working. I fixed that but added a secret short circuit to destroy it once it reached full power; I thought I could create a distraction then rescue Mum and Dad. I didn't think I'd blow the whole place up. I guess it's lucky they weren't there after all!'

Leonora gave a bitter laugh. She leaned her forehead on the leather steering wheel and started to cry. The image she'd seen of her parents in the pod looped around her mind. They'd been stolen from her all over again.

'You know, that was all amazing. *You're* amazing,' said Jack, quietly. Twitchy nuzzled her, squeaking in agreement. She looked at them both at last and wiped her eyes. Then a hesitant smile broke across her face.

She'd done it. She'd stopped her uncle's diabolical plans. She'd saved thousands, maybe *millions* of people from having their happiness stolen. Her parents, wherever they were, would be proud of her. She was proud of herself.

'You know, you're pretty amazing too,' she said. 'You saved my life back there.'

Jack shrugged. 'Well, being a nobody means no one notices me. I snuck off and bumped into *Brenda* of all people. Crazy!'

'Yeah, that was weird. Why was our dinner lady there?' They were both baffled. 'Look, I'm so sorry we argued,' said Leonora. 'And you aren't a nobody, Jack . . . you're the bestest friend *ever*.'

Jack gave her a wonky smile and looked embarrassed, until Leonora broke the awkwardness by punching him on the arm. They burst out laughing.

Over the next few hours, they relived their daring escape as they travelled at full speed back to Crabby Island. The car was a much smoother ride than the submarine (Leonora was itching to dismantle its engine to work out why). And early the next morning she saw a tiny white speck of land appear in the distance. It became

bigger and bigger until –

'Land ahoy! Jack, Twitch!' she cried, nudging them awake.

Jack sat up and rubbed his bleary eyes. Twitchy uncurled himself from her lap. They all stared through the windscreen. Leonora's heart leaped as she saw white sands, sparkling blue lagoons, cliffs topped with swaying yellow grasses. And then she saw – 'Millie!'

Mildred and Captain Spang were standing on the shore next to the beached *Aquabolt*, waving

their arms. Leonora felt an immense rush of relief. She could just make out two other figures standing beside them. It was Professor Insignia and Professor Puri.

Leonora honked the horn and drove right up on to the beach, performing a sand-spraying handbrake turn. She jumped out and into Mildred's waiting arms.

'Oh, me little cherrypie!' murmured Mildred. She scatter-gunned kisses on to Leonora's face. Then she grasped Jack with her spare arm, happily squooozling them both within an inch of their lives.

'Och, thank goodness you're safe,' cried Captain Spang, grinning from ear to ear.

Professor Puri rushed forward and hugged Leonora and Jack too. 'We're so relieved to have you back,' she said, fixing them with her intense look.

Then Professor Insignia stepped forward

182

stiffly and gave them each a formal handshake. 'Indeed, you have displayed the utmost bravery,' he said, his brown eyes twinkling.

Over the next few minutes, Leonora and Jack gabbled about everything that had happened. The incredible underwater lair. Professor Echo's betrayal. Brenda Spaniel's more-than-surprising cameo appearance. And Leonora's parents, who were still being held against their will.

'I still can't believe Kenneth lied to us all,' Mildred said at last, clasping her hands. 'He was Eliza's hero. He'd always used his brilliant mind for good before. Shows how greed can change someone.'

'Sadly, it's often the case,' agreed Professor Insignia, shaking his head. 'I knew we had a spy in our midst, feeding secrets to Luther, disrupting the society's essential work. I would *never* have believed it was him.'

'Nor would I,' said Professor Puri, angrily.

'Such a competent liar, just like your uncle. It's only thanks to *your* incredible talents that he was stopped.'

Leonora felt her face get hot. She opened her mouth to ask several basquillion other questions, but Jack beat her to it.

'Hang on . . . Why was old killjoy Brenda there?' he asked.

Professor Insignia smiled. 'Ah yes, Brenda. She might look like just another busybody, but looks can deceive. She's a secret SIG operative, working from a sleeper cell in Snorebury. Brenda's an expert in the science of camouflage. I tasked her with helping you maintain your low profile in the village. Hence all those rules!'

'Hmph, I knew she didn't have a clue about good cooking,' Mildred muttered, giving Professor Insignia a satisfied nod.

'Or music,' agreed Captain Spang.

'Er, quite,' said Professor Insignia, looking

a little awkward. Then he continued: 'She customized your scooter in record time, Leonora, when you were confronting Luther at the fete. I sent her on ahead to assist with your mission. No one else in SIG knew her undercover identity. I believe she managed to infiltrate the lair disguised as a scientist.'

Leonora frowned. 'So how come she had my Sonic Headmaster Demobilizer?'

'She took it from Miss Clink in the school staffroom,' said Professor Puri. 'Another remarkable invention, Leonora!'

Leonora gave her a half-smile. There was a long pause. The sun dipped behind a cloud. 'Do you think he's still . . . *alive?*' she said at last, a chill creeping along her spine.

'Brenda reported in a few hours ago,' said Professor Puri. 'Unfortunately, she lost sight of Luther in the chaos. If he *is* still alive, I'm afraid he has even bigger plans in play.'

'Bigger plans than controlling human happiness?' Jack gulped.

'We now believe Luther has a global network of secret laboratories operating under the codename Iceheart,' said Professor Insignia.

Leonora swapped looks with Jack. *Iceheart.* She recalled the man who had come looking for her at school and his pale-blue lapel pin. She remembered too the labels on those ghastly inventions in the deep-sea laboratory, each one embossed with a light-blue heart.

'If he has survived,' continued Professor Insignia, 'we'll need your ingenuity to defeat him, Leonora. You know how his mind works. In particular, we think he has some covert projects in the Perilous Desert.'

Leonora's pulse revved. 'Uncle Luther mentioned a desert. That must be where he's got Mum and Dad captive,' she said urgently.

'Then that's where we'll concentrate our

search efforts,' said Professor Puri. 'In the meantime, you must improve Crabby Island's security. We've left a few items in your workshop to help. If he has survived, your uncle Luther might come back here.'

The autumn breeze picked up. Leonora thought she could sense a storm coming. The professors said their goodbyes and started to walk away. When they'd got a little further along the beach, they stopped and Professor Insignia pulled a curious device from his coat pocket. It was Leonora's teleporting Switcheroo.

'An extremely useful gadget,' he said, giving Leonora another smile. He pushed numbers into the device's keypad. Then he and Professor Puri dematerialized.

20
Back to the Workshop

For a long time, everyone stared in silence at the ground where a coffee mug from Professor Insignia's office had been Swticherooed in their place. Then Jack sniffed and said, 'I should be off too. Takes Mum a while to notice I'm gone, but she's bound to be suspicious by now.'

'Don't worry, we'll get a message to her and let her know you're safe,' said Leonora. 'Besides, you can't go yet! We've got work to do.' She glanced up towards the lighthouse, wondering what Professor Insignia and Professor Puri had left up there.

'Aye, guess we need to leave you young'uns to

all that,' said Captain Spang, turning away with a sigh.

'No, you don't,' said Leonora. 'We need your help.'

'We're not much use,' said Mildred, huffily. 'Two washed-up retirees like us. Unemployable, even in *Snorebury*.'

'Are you joking?' said Leonora. 'You heard what Professor Puri said about improving our island security. I need you to get working on some new recipes right away: we need advanced culinary bioweapons!'

Mildred paused, then gave her a beaming smile.

'And, Captain,' Leonora continued, 'you can create an audio artillery – even deadlier than out-of-tune violins.'

Captain Spang's face lit up. 'Aye, I guess I could try,' he said. 'How about I start with my bagpipes, eh?'

'*Bad pipes*, more like,' muttered Jack. Leonora elbowed him in the ribs.

'Perfect,' she said. 'Totally deadly.' With that, they all set off arm in arm towards the lighthouse, excitedly discussing their security plans.

A little while later, Leonora finally clambered up the rickety wooden ladder, wriggled through the hatch and stepped back into her workshop. Hazy sunlight streamed sideways through the great glass roof. She felt her heart leap with excitement – but then she noticed something strange. Her workshop usually looked like an earthquake and hurricane had torn through it hand in hand, but right at this moment it was very nearly . . . *tidy*.

Leonora rushed over to her workbench, which was covered in 4D printers, laptops and all manner of the latest laboratory equipment. New books lined the large wooden shelves.

And on her mahogany desk, glinting in the light, was a golden spanner. It was inscribed with three special letters – SIG. Beside it was a note. Leonora picked it up and read:

Dear Leonora,
Your brilliant imagination is like a superpower. Use it wisely. We'll be in touch again soon.
Best wishes,
Professor Insignia
PS Try not to make any more squirrels glow.

Leonora laughed and pushed the note into her pocket. She picked up the spanner, turning it over in her hands as she walked over to the window. The view outside the lighthouse was dazzling. She could see miles of ocean stretching out in every direction, but already, on the distant horizon, dark clouds were gathering.

As she gazed out, Leonora thought about her parents and about the world beyond, a world that maybe – just maybe – needed someone like her. A little girl with a big imagination, working behind the scenes to defeat the forces of chaos (and sometimes causing a little *extra* chaos as she went about it).

She was, after all, an absolutely extraordinary secret inventor.

Acknowlegements

To write and publish one book is the absolute dream of a lifetime, so I'm as surprised as anyone that they've let me do two.

My heartfelt thanks to all the readers, bloggers, booksellers, librarians and teachers who've championed Leonora so far. I owe you all a mountain of jelly babies.

To my awesome agent, Hannah Weatherill at Northbank Talent, I'm so grateful for all your advice and support. Thank you for being the voice of calm.

Huge thanks to illustrator extraordinaire Gladys Jose for your stunning artwork. Here's hoping we get that dinner together very soon.

I've been so lucky to work with the Puffin Dream Team and especially my incredible editor, Emma Jones. You've made this publishing journey such a joy. Massive thanks also to editorial manager Shreeta Shah for patiently helping to wrangle my words into books.

Thanks to PR and marketing superstars Charlotte Winstone and Mhari Nimmo, Jessica Otway in production, as well as designers Andrea Kearney, Ben Hughes, Ken de Silva and Sean Williams. I'd also like to thank Gift Ajimokun, Guntaas Kaur Chugh and Akelah Adams for your brilliant feedback.

Love and sequins to my gang of amazing, inspiring women. You all rock.

To my kids, nieces and nephews – keep on making me laugh and letting me steal your funny phrases for my stories. Mum, Dad, D, D, L, M and J – don't turn up missing.

Finally, love to Will. Bookshelf builder, graphic designer, publishing cheerleader. Now stick the kettle on. x

Discover how
the adventure
began in . . .

Out now!